a
Pride & Prejudice
story

A P&P Mashup

McKinley James

a

Pride & Prejudice

story

Never let the fear of striking out keep you from playing the
game.

— BABE RUTH

We all wear masks [...]
 we hide from the world
 and from ourselves
 we hide from our truths
 behind our eyes
 running away from our real
 but somewhere there
 where truth meets courage
 we are waiting to be found [...]

— ATTICUS, *LOVE HER WILD*

Prologue

"YOU CAN LEARN a lot from fairytales, you know."

Lizzy Bennet eyed the thick volume of classic fairytales in her father's lap with the kind of skepticism a precocious ten-year-old excels at before turning the same look on her father.

"Like what?" she asked, her tone carrying a hint of curiosity.

Lizzy thought fairytales were for girls—she knew she *was* a girl, but that didn't stop her from trying to be one of the boys. She was always trying to prove she could do all the things they could, in the hopes they'd stop saying girls were dumb and wimpy. She particularly liked baseball, and she was proud whenever they played in gym class, and all the boys backed up when she came up to bat.

"Well." Thomas Bennet scratched at the stubble on his jaw, mulling the question over. "Kindness is a big lesson, for starters. In fairytales, those who are always kind or learn to be kind, even to those who hurt them, always live happily ever after."

"And the bad guys get punished!"

"Yes, they do," he nodded. "The bad guys don't always get punished in real life, but that doesn't mean kindness isn't important. If anything, that makes it more important."

Lizzy trailed a finger down the page the book was open to—a pretty colored sketch of Cinderella's castle at the end of the tale. Her father noticed, and smiled.

"Cinderella is one of my favorites. Know why?"

"Why?" Lizzy automatically scrunched her nose. Cinderella was so girly.

And part of her wondered if her dad chose to read her *Cinderella* because of her new stepmom and stepsisters. She got the feeling they didn't like her, but Dad didn't seem to notice— instead, he probably noticed that *she* didn't really like *them*. She'd *tried* to be nice to them, but they weren't nice back no matter what she did, unless Dad was around.

"Because her kindness is her strength," he explained. "She could easily become bitter with the way she's treated by her step-family, or give in to hopelessness, but she doesn't do either of those things. Some people consider her weak, that she lets her stepmother and sisters walk all over her; maybe sometimes she does, because she's still learning her worth, but she never lets it get to her. Her eventual defiance is quiet, which makes it all the more powerful."

"So..." This time Lizzy scrunched her nose in thought. "She's your favorite because she stands up to the evil stepmother without hurting anyone? And she's still nice to people even though her life was terrible?"

"Yep."

"But that's not fair!" The injustice of it burst out of her as she thought again of her stepmom. "Nothing happens to the stepmother or sisters. They don't get punished."

Mr. Bennet grinned at his daughter, appreciating her. Not all kids her age enjoyed discussing literature. "In this version of the story, they don't—at least not in an obvious way."

"What do you mean?"

"The evil stepmother doesn't win," he pointed out. "She fails to break Cinderella down, and she fails to capture the prince for her own daughters; she doesn't get what she wanted. And she has to live with that failure, and the shame of her treatment of Cinderella—if she's able to feel shame."

Lizzy considered this response before accepting the argument with a nod. "What happens in other versions of the story?"

Thomas chuckled. "When you're a little older, I'll introduce you to the Brothers Grimm."

She perked up. "Grim? That sounds cool."

He grimaced a little as he closed the book. "You may not think so when you read it. Stick to the less gruesome stories for now."

Lizzy pouted, and he kissed the top of her head, then tapped the cover of the book he held for good measure.

"I promise, this book has everything you need inside it."

One

IT IS a truth universally acknowledged that a teenage girl must be in want of a ball.

However little known the feelings or views of such a girl may be when the date of the Netherfield High homecoming dance is announced, it is, regardless, a truth so well fixed in the minds of the surrounding students that it is considered the event of the season.

Lizzy Bennet stood in the kitchen making her stepsisters' lunches for the school day while they sat at the kitchen island. She listened to them gossiping about who would ask whom to the dance with a mix of bemusement and resignation.

It wasn't that she didn't want to go—she would love to put on a nice dress, drink school-sanctioned punch, dance, and take ridiculous photos with her friends. It was that her stepmother was unlikely to allow her to go.

According to Frances Gardiner, there was always something that needed doing, whether it be around the house, or at their family-owned café.

Her dad's café, Lizzy thought, shuddering at the knowledge of what Frances had done to it. That, it was best not to dwell on.

"Hey, that's my scrunchy!" Kitty shrieked. "Give it back!"

"No way," Lydia scoffed. "It looks better on me."

It's literally a scrunchy, Lizzy thought, rolling her eyes as an argument ensued. But bickering seemed to be what the fraternal twins did best.

Kitty, the older twin by fourteen minutes—a fact she loved to lord over her sister—had brown eyes and a round face. Her hair was a mass of thick, dark blonde curls that she straightened to within and inch of its life every day. In contrast, Lydia was all sharp angles, and had the height to go with it. Though she, too, had brown eyes, her hair was a luscious mahogany, naturally straight— a fact she loved to rub in Kitty's face.

Vain, idle, ignorant, and spoiled, they were both juniors, and yet they had all the maturity of a pair of feuding fifth graders.

Less than a year, Lizzy told herself. She only had to put up with them, with all of it, for the remainder of her senior year. Then she was home free.

Once she was done with the lunches, she packed them up in the girls' fancy, shiny lunch totes, plopped them down on the island in front of them while they continued to argue. Then she slid the egg white and anchovy omelet she had warming in the oven out, placed it on a tray with a green smoothie, and, holding her breath so as not to breathe in the fishy scent, carried it upstairs.

Her stepmother was already awake, sitting up in bed when Lizzy entered the room; her sleep mask was pushed up her forehead, making some of her bleached blonde hair bend at odd angles.

"It's about time you showed up," was all she said.

Lizzy made no reply, as there was no point. She simply went to the small round dining table by the window, set the tray atop the lacy table runner. Then she went to the closet, pulled a fluffy pink robe from a hanger on the door, and walked to the bed.

Having removed her sleep mask, Frances sat primly, waiting

impatiently as Lizzy made her rounds. As Lizzy neared the bed, Frances slipped the covers aside—revealing a skimpy, unnecessarily lacy pink negligee—stuffed her feet into hot pink slippers, and rose.

Lizzy held open the robe, and Frances turned, sliding her arms in. As she tied the robe, she ordered, "Spray." Lizzy picked up an essential oil mist spray from the night stand, spritzing the air when Frances turned.

When Frances had inhaled to her satisfaction, she walked to the table and sat down.

"Are these the special anchovies that I ordered?" she asked, cutting into the omelet.

"Yep."

She took a bite, nodded. "Mm. Yes, I can taste the quality. It cost a small fortune, you know."

Lizzy said nothing, but on the inside she rolled her eyes. Frances never bought her own groceries, and never cooked anything for herself—she considered it beneath her. *I could have poisoned the omelet*, Lizzy surmised, *and she wouldn't be able to tell.*

But of course, if she poisoned Frances, she would be the most obvious suspect.

"Did you book my manicure for today?"

"Yes, it's at ten."

"Good." Frances sniffed. "I'm having lunch with Mrs. Long and I'd hate not to look presentable."

Lizzy stood, awaiting further instructions. After a few moments, Frances glanced at her and frowned. "Don't just stand there. Lay out my clothes."

Frances instructed her what items she wanted to wear, and Lizzy pulled them from the closet, laid them on the bed. When Frances finally dismissed her, she stepped quietly out of the room.

Once she'd shut the door, she rushed up the attic stairs to her room.

She shut her own door and leaned against it, taking a moment to breathe. Once she'd reigned in her frustration, she started gathering her things for the day: the textbooks, note-books, and her laptop from her desk all went into her leather messenger bag, then she tossed on a green plaid blazer from the bohemian-style rack that served as her closet, and her phone in its wallet case went from her nightstand to the jacket's inside pocket.

Every personal item she owned was either something she'd had since before her dad died—like her bedroom furniture, her books (and his books), her mother's jewelry, some keepsakes—or some-thing she'd bought with her own money from working at the café.

Most of her clothes, like the jacket she wore, were thrifted, as were any books she'd bought since, with the exception of birthday and Christmas gifts from her friends. Frances had offered to buy her a cheap cell phone and add her to the family plan since she needed to be able to contact her, but Lizzy hadn't wanted to be beholden to her, so she'd saved up her money and bought her own phone.

What Frances didn't know, was the café's manager, Charlotte Lucas—who had also been her mother's best friend—had added Lizzy to her plan. And once Lizzy had turned eighteen—just a few weeks ago—Charlotte had also driven Lizzy to the bank so she could remove France's name from her accounts.

When she was a kid, her father had started savings and checking accounts for her, though she hadn't been able to get a debit card until a few years ago. She was lucky Frances hardly ever paid attention to that account. As Lizzy's guardian, she'd been added as a necessity when Lizzy's dad died. Every once in a while, she'd bought some frivolous thing with money from that account, just to remind Lizzy she could, but for the most part, she left it alone.

Lizzy had been able to save enough for her laptop, the most expensive item she owned. It wasn't necessary at school, but she always took it with her when she left the house because the twins weren't above snooping in her room, sometimes taking her things. She'd learned to hide anything they might consider pretty, and she'd bought a special lamp with a hollow bottom where she hid a cash stash for emergencies.

Another addition she'd eventually made to the room was a deadbolt lock; she kept the key on her house key ring, which she snatched from its place on a hook near the door before turning to scan the room for anything she'd forgotten.

All set, she thought, then headed down to the kitchen to grab her own lunch bag. The kitchen was blessedly empty, so she poured herself a second cup of coffee to enjoy while she waited for Jane.

Lizzy didn't have a car—Frances certainly wouldn't buy her one, and she decided she'd rather save for college for now; she'd worked hard in school and applied to her dad's alma mater, Brown University, but even with a scholarship it would be expensive. So, she caught a ride to school with her best friend, Jane.

Jane was a shy but sweet soul, and loyal as a golden retriever; they'd stuck together through thick and thin since elementary school, the thickest being Lizzy's dad's death eight years past.

She'd sipped about half her mug when Jane texted she'd arrived, so Lizzy gulped down the rest of her coffee, put the mug in the dishwasher, and headed out.

"Good morning!" Jane said cheerily as Lizzy pulled open the passenger door of her yellow Beetle. It wasn't the first time Lizzy thought the car was just as cheerful as her friend.

"Hey," Lizzy smiled, taking in her friend's effortless ensemble.

Effortless, because Jane didn't care much for fashion trends, and because she was easily the most beautiful girl in school.

She had waves of honey blonde hair, which were currently piled into a messy bun, revealing the streak of teal on one side, and big, brown doe eyes with long lashes. Her looks drew eyes wherever she went, but sadly, most of the boys at school paid little attention to her when they realized she actually had a brain in her head.

It made no sense to Lizzy. Jane was beautiful, sweet, and smart, yet a lot of guys thought Jane should only be the first two, and were disappointed to realize she was a nerd.

A hot nerd, but a nerd nonetheless.

But Jane didn't want to be a brainless trophy girlfriend. She loved video games, and wanted to design her own someday. But even some of the nerdy boys tended to avoid her, either because they were overprotective of the gaming industry as a purely male endeavor, or they were too intimidated by someone pretty and, in Lizzy's opinion, cool as Jane.

Jane didn't let it get to her, though. She often displayed her love of video games with t-shirts and pins on her backpack. Today she wore a light pink pleated skirt with a green tee sporting Link from *The Legend of Zelda*.

They chatted on the drive to school, and Jane offered to drop Lizzy off at the café after school so she wouldn't have to walk. Though Lizzy reiterated she liked to walk, she accepted the offer.

Netherfield High's halls were already humming with activity when they arrived, heading straight for their lockers.

Part of the reason they'd always been friends was because their last names both started with B-E-N, and so they'd always been placed next to each other in alphabetically ordered lines, and their cubbies and lockers had always been right next to each other. Little Lizzy Bennet had been skeptical of Jane Benson's bubbly demeanor at first, but she'd easily been won over when Jane shared her snacks.

Snacks were still sacred between the two of them.

Lizzy stuck her lunch in her locker and switched out a couple of her books for those of her morning classes while Jane did the same. When she closed her locker, she jolted, as she hadn't expected a person to be standing on the other side of the door.

"Oh." Reminding herself to be polite, she said, "Hello, Colin."

Tall and lean, all gawky limbs and pointy angles, Colin Hunt gave her an awkward bow and a smile that was all teeth. "Good morning, Elizabeth. Looking lovely, as always."

"Thanks."

He was a nice enough guy, if a little oblivious. He'd moved to the area the previous year, and his favorite thing in the world was Doctor Who, a show Elizabeth enjoyed as well; she'd once made the mistake of wearing a tee with the famous "wibbly wobbly, timey wimey stuff" quote from the episode "Blink."

He'd been convinced they were soulmates ever since.

He was about to speak again when a strangely morphed, zapping sound filled the air. The sound became louder when Colin pulled his phone from his pocket, and Lizzy recognized the ring tone as the sound of the Doctor's sonic screwdriver.

"Pardon me, I have to take this," he apologized, and hurried off.

"Saved by the sonic," Lizzy muttered.

"Lizzy," Jane admonished. "Be nice."

"I was nice. I said hello, and I didn't tell him to buzz off."

Jane only shook her head, and they walked off to head to their first classes.

At lunch they met at their favorite spot in the courtyard, a picnic table under one of the trees. It was in a corner, mostly away from the other tables, and perfectly shaded by the tree. The only thing not in its favor, at least, for Lizzy, was its view of the fountain on the other side.

The table by the fountain was where the Brat Pack sat.

So dubbed by Lizzy because they reminded her of the "cool kids" from 80s movies, this particular group made up of some of the most popular people in school really were a pack of brats. Wealthy and spoiled, Lizzy considered them the epitome of the popular, pampered rich kid cliché.

The worst of them all was Caroline Bingley, head cheerleader and first-rate snob who considered herself to be a queen, and demanded everyone treat her as such. Her lackeys, Anne and Louisa, were also cheerleaders, and were always glued to Caroline's side.

Then there were the guys. All on the Wolves' football team, of course.

Ricky Fitzwilliam, the self-proclaimed ladies' man, was more bark than bite, his bark being an overabundance of teasing. Unfortunately for his romantic aspirations, his teasing fell short of the shameless flirtation mark, and came across as either smug or mocking.

Caroline's twin brother, Charlie, was a surprisingly nice guy, who always had a smile for everyone. Lizzy had often caught him staring at Jane, like he was now; but he'd never asked her out, and neither did he stand up against his sister or his friends.

And then there was Darcy.

Will Darcy: Scion of one of the wealthiest business owners in the area, star quarterback, and notoriously rude. He was, objectively, one of the hottest guys in school, with his perfectly mussed dark hair, piercing green eyes, and rockstar face. But he usually ruined his brooding image the moment he opened his stupid mouth.

In all her years, Lizzy had never met someone as arrogant as

Will Darcy. And yet, he was also an enigma; someone as hot and popular as him could have his choice of any girl, and yet he refused to date anyone.

She'd heard of a few hook ups of his, but on the whole he made it clear he wasn't interested in getting attached to anyone at Netherfield High.

Much to Caroline Bingley's dismay. She liked to think of Will as hers, and was constantly fawning over him, but he mostly ignored her, which was often amusing to watch.

Unfortunately, Lizzy didn't realize she'd been staring at their table, or that Jane had been staring back at Charlie; Louisa noticed, and scrunched up her nose, gesturing to her and Jane with her hands as she spoke to her friends.

Caroline turned and gave them an *I'm-better-than-you* smile. "Why don't you take a picture, freaks?"

"Hey, Coffee Girl?" Ricky called. "Could I get a pumpkin spice latte?"

The remark got some giggles from the group, except Charlie, who shook his head, and Will, who neither smiled nor acknowledged Lizzy and Jane, just kept scrolling through his phone.

Lizzy only rolled her eyes and took a bite of her apple. "They always think everything is about them, don't they? That they're just *so cool*."

"I don't know," Jane said, sighing a little. "I don't think they're all so bad."

Lizzy knew without looking that Jane was talking about Charlie. She'd had a crush on him for years, but was content to admire him from afar.

"Whatever you say."

As if to prove Lizzy's point, Caroline continued, "Where'd you get that grody blazer, Eliza? A thrift store?"

She and her friends chuckled again, but Lizzy raised a brow.

"As a matter of fact, I did. And aside from the fact thrifting is fun, affordable, and good for the environment, I happen to think a Ralph Lauren jacket for ten bucks is a pretty good deal."

Caroline's smile turned brittle, and her friends' laughter immediately cut off. Lizzy wasn't sure if it was because Caroline had inadvertently insulted a designer's taste, or because her barb hadn't landed, but either way, the angry confusion on her face was amusing.

"Whatever," Caroline finally said, turning back to her group.

On the table, Lizzy's phone buzzed, and when she saw who the message was from, her smile bloomed.

"Let me guess," Jane smirked. "The secret admirer."

"He's not an admirer," Lizzy protested. "He's a pen pal."

"Whatever you say," Jane mimicked, and bit into a Flaming Hot Cheeto—their personal favorite snack.

Lizzy stuck out her tongue at her friend, stole one of Jane's Cheetos, then applied herself to responding to Closet Poet's text.

@TheClosetPoet. was the handle of his Instagram account, where he anonymously posted both his favorite poems by other writers, and his own beautiful poetry. He'd discovered her own anonymous account, *@TheLitFairy*, DM'd her to tell her how much he'd liked one of the book quotes she'd posted, and they'd struck up a friendship.

Eventually they exchanged numbers, and often spent the evening hours chatting away about books, life, their struggles.

Everything.

Recently, though, he'd started texting her during school hours, especially the lunch hour. Although both their profiles indicated their pronouns and that they were from the Los Angeles area, and they'd established their ages after a few weeks of messaging so as not to make the friendship weird, it had taken them longer to establish where they went to school.

It simply hadn't been on their radar, but during an instance when they realized they were talking about the same teacher, they'd been ecstatic to learn they went to the same high school. (The teacher in question was Mr. Rothman, a biology teacher known by the students as Moth Man for his insect obsession.)

Smiling at the recollection, Lizzy checked her texts.

CLOSET POET

How are you today?

> Oh, you know. Rolling my eyes at the antics of 'the beautiful people.'

Careful. You're going to make yourself dizzy with all the eye-rolling you do.

> Lol. Old habits die hard.

I wish I could hear your laugh.

Her heart fluttered a little at this admission.

> Maybe you have. Maybe we've met.

As she sent the text, the bell sounded. "Crap," she muttered, hurrying to gather her things. She gathered her bag and rose, tossed her trash. When she turned to join Jane, Will bumped into her on his way into the building, nearly knocking her over.

"Sorry," he mumbled, his eyes glued to his phone, and kept walking.

Jerkwad, Lizzy thought. At least she knew Closet Poet would never be so inattentive.

Two

Maybe we've met.

Those three words had been stuck in Will's head all day.

Of course, the idea he might know Lit Fairy had crossed his mind before—many times since they'd discovered they went to the same school. But for some reason, her voicing the idea was a bit of a revelation. Their school had a few thousand students, but all of a sudden the possibility he may have encountered her before was hitting home.

He'd spent the past couple classes unconsciously looking for her, glancing around at all the faces of his classmates, or absently scanning the crowded halls. He didn't even realize he was doing it until his last class of the day, AP Lit, when Elizabeth Bennet plopped down in her assigned seat next to him, and he automatically trailed his eyes over her face as if searching for a clue. He'd never noticed she had such long lashes before, or a handful of pale freckles dotting her cheeks.

He'd always thought she had an interesting face, but really looking at her now, he realized she was actually pretty cute.

"See something you dislike?" she grumbled.

"What?"

"You're scowling at me." She turned and looked him right in the eye, and the vibrant blue—almost violet—of her irises struck him. "Staring at me like my face offends you."

He blinked, unsure he'd heard her correctly. "*What?*"

She laughed, the sound hollow and humorless, before looking away, shaking her head. She'd pulled out her notebook and a pen, set them on her desk by the time he'd straightened his thoughts. He leaned toward her a little.

"I didn't realize I was staring at you," he murmured. "But I promise it wasn't to criticize. My mind was just wandering."

"Your distinct Darcy frown says otherwise."

"Ha." He could feel his lips twitching. "You can ignore that. It's just my thinking face."

She looked at him now, her brows lifting in exaggerated surprise. "And here I was thinking you were generally displeased by everything. But it turns out you just have resting grump face. Silly me."

He froze, the smile that had been forming slowly turning on itself; he opened his mouth, but was saved from a reply when the teacher rose to begin class. As he turned to face the board, he rubbed at his chest, where it burned a little.

Because the thing was, he *was* generally displeased. Not by everything, exactly, but by his life. His circumstances.

Elizabeth Bennet was perceptive, and she'd hit the mark, but even she likely had no idea just how true her statement had been.

He'd vented his frustrations and resentment to no one but Lit Fairy—not even Charlie, his best friend, knew. How pressured he felt—by the student body, by his friends, and especially his dad—to fit into the role assigned to him.

The school expected him to be the popular football player, date the popular cheerleader, and stick to the "status quo." His dad wanted him to go to Stanford on a football scholarship, study accounting, then come home and eventually take over the family accounting firm.

But he wasn't interested in any of that. He liked football well enough, but he wasn't interested in playing it beyond high school. And he hated math. He wanted to be a writer. The positive response he'd gotten to his original poems he'd posted on his Closet Poet account had only convinced him more that he needed to write.

Caroline Bingley had been insisting the two of them would be perfect together for the last few years, but he'd always found her to be a source of irritation, and it felt like she didn't really like *him* so much as what he represented. He only tolerated her because she was his best friend's sister.

She'd been hinting incessantly he should ask her to the home-coming masquerade, something he would never do, though he was pretty sure she was telling anyone who would listen that he would; she even had their costumes picked out. He might consider it a favor to his friend to dance with her at the dance, but he'd never ask her to be his date—that would give her the wrong idea. Besides, who he really wanted to ask was Lit Fairy.

It grated to feel like he had no say in his own life.

But it helped to know Lit Fairy felt similarly about her own life —he knew her parents had died some years ago, and she'd mentioned her demanding stepmom and spoiled stepsisters. Always running around doing errands for them, catering to their whims.

He hoped talking to him gave her some relief.

He decided to ask her if that was the case when he texted her later that evening.

LIT FAIRY

What do you mean?

> I know it's out of the blue, I was just thinking today about how we both feel the lack of control over our lives. I always feel better when I talk to you, and I wondered if you felt the same.

Her response came quickly.

In that case, yes, you do bring me relief.

> I'm glad. You're the only one I feel like myself around. I don't have to wear a mask with you.

This time her response didn't come for nearly a minute, but finally she said:

I know exactly how that feels.

A thought struck him then, as he recalled the suggestion they'd met without realizing it, and his wishing he could just ask her to the dance. Inspired, he wrote:

> A mask wears many faces
>
> our eyes fail to recognize
>
> but the discerning heart can see
>
> through any sort of disguise.

🙂 Did you just write that? What brought this on?

> I want to meet you, ironically while wearing a mask—at the homecoming masquerace.

Do you think that's a good idea? What if the
magic of this is in the mystery?

> I do. The best part of a mystery is solving it. I
> want to meet you.

He waited nearly five minutes before her reply finally came,
and he held his breath as he opened the message.

Then I'm in.

He released the breath and smiled, considering. The dance was
from seven to ten, but it would probably be complicated to try to
meet up right away.

> I have it on good authority there will be a disco
> ball above the dance floor. Meet me under it at
> 9 p.m.?

I'll see you there.

Grinning like an idiot, he left her with one last message.

> Can't wait.

In a daze, Lizzy pocketed her phone. Closet Poet had just asked to
meet her in person.

And she'd agreed.

Granted, the whole point of a masquerade was to hide your
identity with a mask, but meeting in person would undoubtedly
make everything more...real.

Did she want it to be real?

Though she'd never named names, or mentioned her job, Closet Poet knew about her dad's death and her dysfunctional stepfamily. But was it courting disaster for him to witness her servitude in action? She'd make sure he and Frances or the twins never met, of course; she couldn't imagine Frances would want her dating anyone, so it would have to be a secret. He might not be willing to do that.

He might potentially be willing to wait until graduation, but that was several months away. And everything would change once they both went off to college.

"For Pete's sake," she muttered under her breath, automatically scooping the dishes from empty tables as she walked around with a bus bin. "You are way overthinking this, Lizzy."

She'd said the last as she brought the full bin behind the counter, heading into the kitchen.

"What was that?" Charlotte turned from the register and raised a neatly plucked brow, her dark brown eyes all-knowing. Though she had to wear Frances's mandated uniform of bubble gum pink apron with frilly white hems, which stood out against her cocoa powder skin, it was always pressed and clean, and her glossy dark curls were always pulled back in an impeccable ponytail, a French braid on either side of her temples.

"Oh, nothing, just berating myself for thinking of ways something could end before it even begins." Instead of shrugging, Lizzy adjusted the bin, which was starting to get heavy.

"Oh, of course." Charlotte smiled like this was usual—which it pretty much was—and shook her head while Lizzy brought the bin to the sink in the kitchen. "Now, what are you still doing here?"

In addition to being the manager, Charlotte had been a close friend of Lizzy's mom. She'd been a presence in her life from nearly the day Lizzy was born, and was the only real mother-figure she'd ever known. Lizzy had to admit, when she was a kid she'd hoped maybe Charlotte and her dad would fall in love and get married, and then Charlotte would be her real mom.

But that was one of many dreams that had ended when he'd died, along with taking over the family business when she grew up.

The café had once been *Bookish Brews*, an open, airy space with a light industrial design inspired by the brick wall shared with the shop next door. There'd been bright Edison bulbs, an art wall, a comfortable rug, tables for people to sit and work or eat at, and a cozy area with plush chairs if they'd rather sit and chat or read.

Of course, there'd also been an old sideboard filled with second-hand paperbacks that people could choose from if they desired. And there'd been a little stage where they had readings and open mic nights.

They'd served fresh gourmet coffee from hand-picked vendors, and made artisanal book-themed drinks, including Thomas Bennet's custom tea blends. Their menu had included fun, delicious baked goods, and hearty sandwiches and soups.

Now it was *Frances's*—what gall to rename the place after herself, Lizzy thought—and was hardly a shadow of its former iteration.

The square wooden tables had been replaced with smaller round ones, and covered up with delicate lacy tablecloths, topped with a statuette of Aphrodite as the centerpieces; the functional chairs were now white metal bistro chairs with heart-shaped backs and frilly, leopard print cushions.

The stage and the lounge area with the books was gone, and instead there were more garishly decorated tables there. The deco rug had been replaced by a shag rug with a pink and white zebra stripe pattern. Neon pink curtains hung in the windows, and the art had all been swapped out for prints Lizzy found strange—a swan flapping its wings, a plush pink teddy bear with a mug of coffee, a close up of a woman's foot wearing a neon pink high heel.

All in all, a cohesive design it was not—basically, Frances had used redecorating as an excuse to inflict her personal style on everyone, adding frills and lace wherever possible.

It was like a textile factory had barfed up its scrap fabrics directly on top of the old design.

As for the food, that had been a near disaster. Frances had also tried to make the café a go-to spot for all the latest weird diet trends, and the customers loyal to the original Bookish Brews had revolted. So now, they still served some of their original items, but added smoothies and salads to the menu, and sold overpriced bottles of sparkling water at the register.

Lizzy had nothing against salad or smoothies; in general it wasn't a bad addition. But every month there was a special of some kind determined by Frances—like seaweed pancakes, sardine casserole, or a peanut butter and anchovy smoothie to name a few.

Lizzy was sure the original menu, including the coffee vendors they'd managed to keep, was what was keeping the business afloat.

And Charlotte had been there through it all, as had Mary, their chef, Maddie, another server and back-up cook, and Maddie's husband, Ed, server and dishwasher.

Lizzy was grateful for them all. Other than Jane, they were her only family.

When she came back out of the kitchen, Charlotte had her hands on her hips, the still-unanswered question clear on her face.

"You know Frances will throw a fit—"

"Your shift ended ten minutes ago." Stern but kind, Charlotte merely tilted her head. "Now get out of here. I'm sure you've got homework—scoot!"

"Okay, okay." Lizzy help up her hands. "I'm gone."

She removed her pink apron, grabbed up her bag, and offered

a farewell smile to Charlotte and the others before walking the few blocks to the one place Frances would never think to find her.

She stayed at the library until it closed at nine, completing her homework for the next day, and getting a head start on other assignments before taking time to read for pleasure.

"He wants to meet you?"

Jane's giddy smile had not a few heads turning in their direction in the hall as they walked it the next morning. Most everyone wore school colors—black and red—in anticipation of the homecoming game, and Lizzy was grateful she thought to wear a red t-shirt so she didn't stand out too much.

Lizzy still couldn't quite believe it herself, even though she'd struggled to fall asleep thinking about it. She'd never expected Closet Poet to want to meet her in person, but in hindsight that had been silly. Once they'd realized they went to the same school, it was probably inevitable they'd meet. She allowed a small smile as they walked, and whispered, "Yep. At the dance."

"That's so exciting!" Jane practically squealed. "We have to find you the most amazing costume. Do you know what you want to be?"

High-pitched, hyena-like laughter upbraided their ears from just in front of them, and they turned to see Lydia prancing toward them, Kitty close behind.

"Don't tell me I just heard what I think I heard." Lydia snorted so hard Lizzy was surprised she didn't pull a muscle. "You're planning to go to the dance?"

Great. Just what she needed.

"Maybe," she shrugged, answering before Jane could. Sweet

Jane was naive enough to think Lydia and Kitty would be supportive of the idea. "I haven't decided yet."

"Don't you have to work?" Kitty asked.

"No, I don't have a shift tomorrow," Lizzy admitted, knowing better than to tell them it was her first day off in months. She decided to add a layer to her mask, hoping to distract them from their purpose. "I may use the extra time to write an extra credit essay."

As expected, Lydia scoffed. "Nerd. Whatever, it's not like it matters. Mom would never let you go the dance anyway."

She and Kitty giggled as they continued down the hall. Jane glanced after them, worrying her bottom lip.

"You don't think they'll tell Frances, do you?"

Lizzy only sighed. "What do you think?"

The rest of the school day was blissfully uneventful; she even managed to avoid Colin. She and Closet Poet didn't talk, but she imagined they were both thinking about the dance and the possibilities it might bring. Without realizing it, she found herself smiling; the twins and Frances might try to ruin her plans, but they could never take away what she and Closet Poet had. Despite the sense of foreboding, she remained in a good mood throughout the day.

She wasn't the only one, she noticed. In AP Lit, Will looked pretty happy himself, surprising her by directing a small smile her way when she took her seat next to him.

She quirked a brow. "Darcy."

"Bennet." He nodded back before turning his attention to the front.

She replayed Closet Poet's words from the night before.

I don't have to wear a mask with you.

Elizabeth knew exactly what he meant. It was exhausting, pretending not to be bothered by, or even angry with, Frances or the twins. To do everything they asked without complaint when what she really wanted was to yell at them. To tell them what she really thought of them. To call them out for everything they'd done.

She also felt the same—there were things she'd told Closet Poet she hadn't even told Jane. They weren't secrets, but Jane was too soft-hearted to understand her frustration. Maybe she didn't give her friend enough credit, but it was easier to vent to her secret pen pal, perhaps because she had no face or real name to put the words to. So she often kept the worst of Frances's demands and antics from Jane and Charlotte, knowing one would get upset, and the other would be angry enough to want to do something, and she'd rather avoid the drama.

Maybe it was some kind of fate they met online, allowing them to get to know each other without preconceived ideas about each other.

At the end of the day, she and Jane had some free time before Lizzy had to work, so they took their softball gear out to the vacant field. Jane was a pitcher on the school softball team, and as much as Lizzy would have liked to join her, Frances had been adamant she'd never allow it. Not just because she didn't want to put money toward a hobby of Lizzy's, but because she believed no girl should play a sport so dirty and unruly.

After warming up, Jane set a small bucket of balls next to the mound while Lizzy took her stance at the plate.

"Are you worried about tomorrow?" Jane bent to choose a ball.

"I'm probably more nervous than I'm letting myself feel right now." Lizzy readied her bat. "I've deliberately not been thinking about what could go wrong."

Jane wound up, released the ball; Lizzy swung, smacked a

grounder between third and second. "Do you think he won't like you when you meet in person?"

"I mean, I doubt I'll be what he's expecting."

Lizzy shrugged, retook her stance. It wasn't like she'd suddenly be a different person, and Closet Poet would know that. But if they had met before, if he didn't have a positive opinion of Lizzy Bennet, she imagined it might be hard to accept.

Jane threw another pitch, and this time Lizzy sent it over her head into center field.

"And you?" Jane paused with the next ball in her hand. "Are you afraid you'll be disappointed?"

"I...hadn't considered that, actually." She didn't think she would be disappointed, unless Closet Poet turned out to be Colin, or someone like Ricky Fitzwilliam. Or Charlie Bingley, since she would never interfere in Jane's crush.

In her distraction, she swung too late at the next pitch, fouled it off—and felt her pocket buzz. "Sorry," she said to Jane as she pulled it out. Thankfully it was a text, not a call.

"Frances," she told Jane. "She wants me to pick up her special brand of sunscreen for her Saturday sunbathing."

"Why do you put up with her crap?" Jane asked, surprising Lizzy with her vehemence.

"It's just easier," Lizzy reminded her. "If I openly disobey her edicts, or put up a fuss, she has the power to make my life miserable."

"You're a legal adult now, Lizzy," Jane pointed out. "The only power she has over you now is the power you give her."

Stunned, Lizzy straightened. "Wow, Jane. That's...profound."

"Don't tease me about this, Lizzy."

"I'm serious." She turned to face her friend. "Your advice is sound, and I'll try to do better. But it'll be hard as long as I still live under her roof."

Frances's roof, not her dad's—a fact she often resented. He probably would have left it to Frances anyway, but since he hadn't left a will, everything went to Frances regardless. She could move out, she acknowledged, but it didn't change the connection she had to the house she grew up in, despite it not being home since he died.

Softening, Jane nodded, held up another ball. "One more?"

"Yeah."

Lizzy bent her knees, choked up on the handle and aligned her knuckles before lifting her bat from her shoulder. As Jane released the ball she imagined Frances's smug face, and swung.

She felt it hit the sweet spot, heard the *ping* of ball meeting metal before the ball sailed into left field. To her astonishment, it dropped on the other side of the fence, near the field where a couple guys were tossing a football around.

"What's that smile for?"

Will shook himself from thoughts of Lit Fairy, tossed the pigskin back to Charlie. They'd decided to play some catch to help dispel their pre-game nerves before heading home for dinner; but Will found that with his mind on Lit Fairy, the homecoming game didn't seem that important. "Just...thinking about a girl," he admitted.

Charlie tilted his head. "I doubt Caroline put that smile on your face. You hardly ever smile around her."

Will grimaced—sometimes it was easy to forget Charlie was Caroline's brother. They were so different. "No. I...I've actually been trying to think of a way to tell her I'm not going to ask her to the dance. Make it clear I'm not interested in her at all."

Charlie whistled, but a smile lit his face. "And how's that going for you?"

"I tried to talk to her at lunch today, but she put me off."

"Sounds about right." Charlie threw the ball back. "She won't let you off the hook easily."

Will frowned. "I've never been on the hook, you know that."

"I do, but she thinks you're soulmates or something. I know that's crap, because she's never bothered to get to know you beyond surface level, but she won't give up the idea of having a rich, popular boyfriend without a tantrum at the very least."

Tantrum sounded like an appropriate word when it came to Caroline.

"I'm aware. I'm sorry in advance for the disturbance to your household."

Charlie waved him off before catching the ball. "Eh. She's gotta learn eventually she can't always get what she wants."

As he threw the ball back, and Will caught it, a scuffed neon yellow softball plopped onto the edge of the field with a distinct *thud*, bouncing a couple times before coming to a halt in the grass. They both glanced at the softball field, where two girls were cheering; the batter in particular was pumping her bat up and down in victory.

"Nice hit." Charlie grinned. "I think that's Jane and Lizzy."

"How can you tell?" Will squinted at the figures on the field, but he couldn't make out any faces—though he did notice the pitcher's blonde hair.

"Well, uh..." Charlie blushed as Will walked over and picked up the softball. "I know Jane pitches for the softball team. And I've heard her and Lizzy talking about practicing together before."

Will lifted a brow, then chucked the ball back over the fence, where it landed in the outfield.

"Thank you!" the batter called, and it did sound a little bit like Elizabeth.

"You're welcome!" he called back.

Three

Saturday morning, Lizzy found Frances already spread out on one of the lounges next to the pool in their backyard, sunning herself like a lazy cat.

You can do this, she told herself, gripping the sunscreen.

"What took you so long?" Frances narrowed her eyes, lowering her enormous, wing-tipped sunglasses.

"Sorry," Lizzy said, trying to placate her.

"Hmph." Frances sat up, thankfully saying no more, and held out her hand for the bottle. Lizzy handed it to her, all the while waiting for the other shoe to drop.

"So, you wanted to talk to me," she started.

Frances squirted what looked like a lake's worth of sunscreen into her palm, began rubbing it over her arms and chest. "Yes. One of the baristas called in sick. I'll need you to take their shift tonight."

And there it was. Maybe someone had called in sick, but employee schedules were Charlotte's purview. Likely Frances had learned she intended to go to the dance from the twins, and was creating an excuse to prevent her from going. Not that she needed an excuse—Frances often ordered her to work when she hadn't been scheduled to, but at least she got extra pay out of it.

"I have tonight off," Lizzy reminded her, hoping she was wrong. "It's been on the schedule for months, and I have plans for tonight."

"I know, but we all have to make sacrifices in life." Now Frances applied the sunscreen to her legs, pouting as though she were actually sorry to disappoint. "I'm afraid you won't be able to go to the homecoming dance."

Gritting her teeth, Lizzy took a breath before responding. "Frances, I do everything that you ask me, and I never ask you for anything. But I'm asking you now, please don't make me work on my night off. I'll work any other extra shift."

She deliberately didn't mention the dance, hoping not to draw attention to it, or how much she wanted to go. But Frances stilled, her frown pronounced as she looked up with a superior glare.

"You need to learn to stop being so selfish, Elizabeth. Having a job is good for you." She ran an appraising eye over Lizzy's messy bun, jeans, and t-shirt before slathering her stomach. "Besides, you're too bookish. You're not plain, but you're not as pretty or lively as the girls, so this job could be all you'll ever have. Why waste your time on a frivolous dance?"

Lizzy fought to control her expression, keeping her face carefully neutral instead of displaying the anger that wanted to boil over. When she said nothing, Frances glanced at her with another frown.

"Understand?" When Lizzy simply nodded, her face brightened into a saccharine smile. "Good. Now come lather my back."

Sanctimonious, hypocritical shrew, Lizzy thought, calmly taking back the bottle. She could point out that Kitty and Lydia, two of the most spoiled, self-centered girls on the planet, had no jobs and were going to the dance. But Frances saw no need for her girls to work, and had raised them to be just as selfish and mean-spirited as she.

An idea struck her as she sat behind Frances, squeezed a bit of sunscreen into her hand. Smirking to herself, she methodically rubbed the white paste onto Frances's back, leaving a few small, strategically placed lines free of coverage.

"All done," she said, trying not to sound gleeful.

"Good. Now go do the laundry." Frances dismissed her and rolled onto her stomach, exposing her back to the sun and untying her bikini straps.

Lizzy strode back into the house, the little spring in her step unnoticed by her tormentor.

Despite the hour, Will considered making a pot of coffee. He thought he might need the kick—though they'd won their homecoming game, it had been a long week, and he was exhausted. Then again, he was nearly giddy with nervous energy.

Tonight, he would meet Lit Fairy in person.

But first he had to clarify to Caroline he was not taking her to the dance, to ask her to back off once and for all. He couldn't help but feel like she knew what he was going to do and was deliberately delaying speaking to him privately, which was irritating. Charlie had been right, of course—she wouldn't give up on him easily.

He'd just have to do it when their group met up later. If she thought the presence of their friends would stop him, she was wrong.

"Lunch is ready."

Their longtime housekeeper, Mrs. Reynolds, poked her head into the living room. "Your sister is in the music room, but I'm not sure where your father is."

"Thanks, Mrs. R. I'll find him."

But first, he'd go get his sister.

Georgianna was in the fifth grade, and smart as a whip. She'd been only five when their mother died, and didn't have any lasting memory of her, but had inherited her love and talent for music. She'd been taking piano lessons for the past few years, and was progressing quickly since she practiced constantly. And for her next endeavor, after becoming obsessed with Lindsay Sterling, she expressed an interest in learning the violin.

Will could hear the rough, scratchy sounds of bow on string performing a scale as he neared the closed music room door. He tapped a knuckle against the wood before opening it to see her standing in the center of the room, violin tucked loosely in the crook of her neck.

"Gianna? Lunch's ready."

"Finally!" Georgianna sagged, letting her arms drop like noodles. "My arms are *so* tired!"

Adoring her, he only chuckled as she set the instrument on its stand. "I remember you saying something similar about your fingers when you started piano lessons. You'll get used to it."

"They still get tired sometimes." Turning, she held up her hands to wiggle her fingers. "And my teacher says the tips of my fingers will get tough. Calsees? Calmooses?"

"Callouses."

"Yeah! And then my fingers won't be so sore." Her eyes—green like his, like their mother's—were wide with excitement, and she reached for the hair band around her wrist, tying her sandy blonde hair—like their father's—into a tail.

She skipped a little as they made their way to the dining room, passing by the stairs, where their father was coming down, a few papers in his hand.

"Oh, hey," Will said. "Mrs. R says lunch—"

"William, what are all these letters for? You applied to other colleges?" Holding up the papers, Robert Darcy strode down the remaining few steps. He didn't look angry, exactly, but he was definitely miffed—probably because Will had never informed him he'd applied, much less been accepted, to colleges that weren't Stanford.

Well, Will was a little miffed himself. Those acceptance letters had been sitting on his desk, the one for his dream school, Brown, right on top.

"Why were you in my room?"

He sounded every bit the petulant teenager, and the look on his father's face told him so. It also demanded an explanation.

Will sighed, not ready for the whole I-don't-actually-want-to-go-to-Stanford talk now. "Look, Dad, all the college guidance counselors advise against only applying to one school. I wanted to have options."

"You don't need options. Your grades are excellent; excel for the rest of the football season, and your acceptance to Stanford is guaranteed." When Will said nothing, and he realized Georgianna was watching them both with wide eyes, Robert cleared his throat and handed the letters back. "I understand following the advice of the counselors, though. I suppose on the off-chance you don't get accepted to Stanford, you'll have backups to choose from."

Without waiting for a response, he walked to the dining room. Irritated, Will stomped up to his room to shove the letters in his desk drawer.

"Why don't you just tell him you don't want to go?"

He looked up to see Georgianna leaning in the doorway, arms crossed. He mirrored her stance.

"What do you know?"

She rolled her eyes. "Please. Like I can't tell you get all grumpy and silent whenever Dad mentions Stanford. And you hate math, so I'm betting you don't want to be an accountant, either."

Kids were a lot smarter than adults tended to give them credit for, Will thought, lips curving into a reluctant smile.

"I'll tell him when I'm ready."

"And when will that be?"

He hesitated. "Soon."

"It better be." She pushed off the door and turned toward the hall, smiled smugly. "Or I'll tell him myself."

He narrowed his eyes, but she was already heading back downstairs. Grumbling to himself, he followed.

He just had to make it through the afternoon, and then he'd see Lit Fairy.

By the time she stepped into the café that afternoon, Lizzy's mood had plummeted. Not only could she not go to the dance, now she had to work on her day off. Charlotte would know about the requirements to get her time off rescheduled, but it would be too late. She'd miss her chance to meet Closet Poet at the dance.

She needed to message him. They could meet another time, without the mystery of the masquerade.

Since the other staff already working had the front covered, she decided to do a bit of inventory. An hour or so into her shift, she was interrupted by Maddie.

"Lizzy, hon, I really have to use the restroom. Do you think you could cover the front for a few minutes?"

"Oh, sure." She set down her clipboard and went out to the counter.

To her unending bad luck and dismay, the Brat Pack walked in a few moments later. Caroline headed the party, strolling up to the counter like she was on a catwalk.

Lizzy put on her best blank customer service face. "Hi, guys. What can I get you?"

Caroline pursed her lips. "I'll have the green fat burning smoothie."

Lizzy resisted the urge to roll her eyes, instead raising a brow. "You know there's actually a ton of sugar in that, right?"

The guys chuckled, while Caroline sneered at her, and her friends just looked confused. "Do you think I'm stupid?" Caroline asked. "Health smoothies don't have sugar added to them."

"Here we go," Will murmured under his breath. If Caroline noticed, she ignored it, instead staring Lizzy down. For her part, Lizzy couldn't help flicking a glance at Will before meeting Caroline's gaze, surprisingly proud she'd made the brooding football player laugh.

"No *added* sugar, yes." Lizzy shrugged. "But fruit has natural sugars, so there's no need to add sugar anyway."

Caroline sniffed, then picked up one of the bottles of fancy sparkling water from their display. "I'll just have this," she declared, setting it on the counter.

"You know," Ricky stepped forward. "I'm still waiting on that pumpkin spice latte, Coffee Girl."

Lizzy gave him a sweet, bland smile. "Would that be for here, or to go?"

He opened his mouth, but Will stepped up before his friend could respond, clapping him on the back.

"He'll take it to go," he told her. "And I'll have a black coffee to go."

Her lips twitched, and she nodded. "Together or separate?" she asked.

"I got it," Will assured his friends, pulling out a credit card.

She almost rolled her eyes—of course he had a credit card. But she took it, arched a brow at him.

"You sure about the pumpkin spice latte?"

He gave her a conspiratorial smirk, lowered his voice so only she would hear. "He secretly enjoys them."

"Got it." She rang him up, handed his card back, then set about making the drinks.

Will watched her for a moment before turning to join his friends, who'd sat down at a nearby table. Caroline patted the open seat next to her, smiling brightly.

"I hope you didn't give her a tip," she remarked when he sat down on the fuzzy leopard cushion.

Tired of her attitude, he stared at an odd picture of a pug in a pink bowtie on the wall of other weird photos. It was now or never.

He turned to her. "You promised me earlier that we could talk."

"Alright, so talk." She sipped casually at her water.

"I meant privately."

"Will, seriously. There's nothing you can't say to me in front of our posse."

He gave her a speculative look, but either she didn't understand, or was just refusing to. Either way, she'd brought it on herself.

He blew out a breath. "Okay. Stop telling people that I'm taking you to the dance, because I'm not."

Her expectant smile dropped like an anvil, Anne and Louisa's mouths gaping open beside her. Ricky let out a guffaw, while Charlie merely looked on with resignation.

"What?" Caroline screeched. "Don't be ridiculous, of course you are."

"No, I'm not. I haven't asked you, and I'm not going to. And furthermore," he continued, "I'm not going to ask you out, either, so please stop hitting on me, and insinuating to others that we're the perfect couple."

"But we *are* perfect together!"

"I disagree. I don't think we're right for each other."

Her expression turned mutinous, but then she deliberately calmed herself, contorted her face into a serene smile.

"I understand you're having some commitment issues, and I forgive you," she said, like he was a child. "The girls and I are going to go get ready for the dance, so you just take your time, think things through, and we'll meet you there. Okay?"

"There's nothing to think through, Caroline." Exasperated, he decided he needed to be more forceful. "I'm not interested in you as anything other than my friend's sister. You and I will never be a thing."

He could tell Caroline was about to give her temper free reign, but before she could respond, Elizabeth called his name from the counter. He rose, his chair squeaking against the floor, and went to get the coffees. He heard Caroline and her friends stomp out the door, and a look over his shoulder informed him Charlie was guiding Ricky to wait outside.

"One black coffee and one PSL, to go," Elizabeth said, her tone deliberately professional. When she pressed her lips together in silent glee, he squinted at her.

"How much did you hear?"

To his surprise, she grinned from ear to ear. He'd never seen her smile like that—at least, not at him. It looked good on her— and made those blue-violet eyes sparkle.

"Enough to make my day," she practically sang.

"Oh, really?" He lifted a brow, leaned an elbow on the counter toward her. "Glad I'm still single, huh?"

Her smile fell away, sending a surprising amount of disappointment through him. "No, jerkwad. I've just never been so delightfully entertained at work, and the memory of Caroline's head about to explode will keep me going for weeks. Maybe even until we graduate."

The wistful look on her face made him snort. Straightening, he picked up the to-go mugs. "Well, glad I could entertain you."

Outside, he handed Ricky his drink and took a sip of his own —it was surprisingly good coffee. Ricky grimaced at the cup in his hand, but took a gulp, and after a few moments, smiled in appreciation.

"So, that went well," said Charlie, a sarcastic smile on his face.

"Sorry for working her up. I'm sure it'll be a while before you hear the end of it."

"Probably, but I'm used to it."

"So you're obviously not going to the dance with Caroline," Ricky said as they started walking. "What are you going to do if you both win homecoming king and queen?"

"Crap. I hadn't thought about that." Will shrugged, though mostly to himself. "Maybe I won't win."

"Fat chance."

Will shook his head. "I guess I'll cross that bridge when I get to it."

Charlotte stepped out of the office when Maddie came back.

"Those kids reminded me why I hated high school," she remarked, appraising Lizzy's smile. "Though the young man flirting with you was very handsome."

"He was *not* flirting with me!" Lizzy sputtered, and reached for a rag to keep her hands busy. The cocky grin Will had given her had, admittedly, fried her brain for a few seconds.

"Mm-hm. If you say so."

Jane came in as Lizzy started wiping down the counter, relieving her from the direction of that conversation.

"Hey," Lizzy greeted her, grateful for the interruption. "Shouldn't you be getting ready for the dance?"

Jane nodded decisively. "Yes—and so should you."

"What's this about a dance?" Charlotte asked.

"Tonight is the homecoming dance," Jane told her. "It's a costume masquerade."

"And Frances demanded I work tonight," Lizzy reminded her.

Charlotte leaned an arm on the counter, placed a hand on her hip. "On your night off, no less."

"It doesn't matter." She knew she didn't sound convincing—probably because she was trying to convince herself. She'd been telling herself it didn't matter all evening, and she'd nearly managed to believe it; but saying it out loud, it sounded hollow as an echo in a cave.

"Doesn't matter?" Jane exclaimed. "What about Closet Poet?"

"Who?" Charlotte narrowed her eyes.

"No one," Lizzy assured her. "He's a guy I met online, and we've been chatting for a while."

"And he asked her to meet him at the dance tonight," Jane revealed, her tone smug.

A slow grin spread over Charlotte's face. "What? Well, now you have to go."

"Hello?" Lizzy gestured around the café. "Frances would literally murder me for defying her. And then make my ghost bury the body."

"Lizzy." In her protective, motherly way, Charlotte laid her hands on Lizzy's shoulders. "When was the last time you went on a date? You know if your father were here, he wouldn't want you to waste your life being at that woman's beck and call. You're eighteen—she doesn't legally have a hold over you anymore."

At Jane's *told you so* look, her shoulders drooped. "If he were here, I wouldn't have to be at her beck and call. And once I graduate, I'll be free of her."

"You want to wait until we graduate to go after true love?" Jane narrowed her eyes, placed her fists on her hips—since she hardly ever got frustrated, Lizzy knew she was serious.

"True love? Jane, come on. This isn't The Princess Bride. Or a Hallmark movie."

"No," Charlotte said gently, brushing some of Lizzy's hair from her face to cup her cheek. "But it is your life. And it breaks my heart to see you set it aside in favor of keeping the peace. You never do anything for yourself."

"Yeah," said Mary, poking her head out of the kitchen. "When you're not running around for Frances, you're always here working, or at the library studying. Why not go do something fun?"

"Trust me, honey," Maddie added. "You don't want to look back on this time and regret not taking a chance on what you want."

She wasn't setting her life aside so much as hiding it—and biding her time, she thought. But she couldn't remember the last time she and Jane had just done something fun for the fun of it. And as for a date, well—the answer to Charlotte's question was never.

"You're right," she nodded, smiling slowly. "I should go."

"Yes!" Jane pumped her fists, and the others beamed in victory.

Lizzy's smile grew wider. She was going to do it; she was going to dress up, and meet Closet Poet, and dance with him, and—

"Oh." Her smile faded quickly. "Wait. I don't have a costume. How am I supposed to go to a costume masquerade?"

"Oh, I got you a mask when I got mine," Jane assured her. "And you don't need anything crazy—do you have a nice dress or something?"

"Maybe, but I can't go back to the house," Lizzy pointed out. "And I won't fit in your clothes."

"Wait." Charlotte gripped Lizzy's shoulder, lips curving in the kind of smile that takes over your face when you have a really good idea. "I think I have just the thing. Maddie, you're in charge."

Charlotte's house was a quaint little bungalow, white with dark green shutters. She'd lived there for as long as Lizzy could remember, and had slowly updated it over the years, making it a comfortable and eclectic home, which she kept immaculately tidy.

Since her dad's death, Lizzy felt more at home there than the house she grew up in. But one place she rarely ventured was the basement, as there was no reason to go down there.

But now she and Jane followed Charlotte down the basement steps, anticipation ramping up her curiosity. She was surprised to see it was semi-finished, with a laundry area, some storage, and a small gym with weights and a treadmill.

Charlotte headed for the storage area, slid an old trunk out from under some shelves. It was probably made of wood, but was covered in dark brown vinyl, its handles and latches a little grimy with time. Flicking the latches open, Charlotte lifted the lid.

Inside were clothes, neatly folded, and a couple of smaller boxes. Charlotte moved a few items aside, then reached in and, almost reverently, pulled out a ballgown.

It was floor length, and strapless but for the loose scoops at the shoulders. The sweetheart neckline was beaded in a shimmering, midnight blue all the way down to the waistline, where layers of tulle tapered out in shades of the same blue and sparkling silver.

"Everything in this trunk was your mother's," Charlotte told her. "She wore this dress to prom."

"Oh, Lizzy." Jane's eyes watered a little. "It's gorgeous."

Lizzy's throat tightened. "Mom wore this?"

With hesitant fingers, she took the dress from Charlotte, held it delicately to her chest. A little teary eyed, Charlotte plucked up one of the smaller boxes. After rummaging around a little, she held out a photograph.

From the image, a much younger Charlotte, dressed in a golden yellow evening gown that brought out the coppery tones in her dark skin, beamed with her arm slung over the shoulders of another young woman. The young woman, Lizzy's mother, had her arm around Charlotte's waist, and was smiling just as brightly.

And she was wearing the blue ballgown.

Lizzy took the photo, swallowed down the tears that wanted to come through the burn in her throat.

"You look so much like her," Charlotte said.

"Charlotte." Lizzy blinked, but one tear escaped. "Thank you. Thank you for keeping these things, and showing them to me now."

"Of course, baby." Charlotte gave Lizzy a quick, tight squeeze. "Now let's get you ready to meet your Prince Charming, Cinderella."

Though she sniffled one more time, the comment had the desired effect of drying Lizzy's tears.

"Cinderella?" Lizzy raised a brow. "Don't you think that's a little on the nose?"

Jane shrugged. "You might as well own it. What about shoes?"

Lizzy shook her head. "I already know my mom's shoes don't fit me. I'd rather wear my Chucks anyway."

"Hm." Jane pursed her lips, but after studying the dress, nodded. "I'm sure the dress will cover your shoes."

Smiling, Charlotte held up a finger. "Oh, and one more thing."

She turned back to the box, plucked up a small jewelry box from the top.

"I know you have some of your mom's jewelry," she explained. "But this bracelet is one I got her as a gift once—your dad gave it back to me when he told me he was going to ask Frances to marry him."

She pulled out a thin gold chain, adorned with little golden roses. Tiny, perfect pearls were nestled in between each rose.

"Would you want to have it?"

Lizzy's eyes welled again, but she didn't notice. "Of course. Thank you, Charlotte."

"You're welcome. Now, let's get you two ready for this dance!"

Four

SHE FELT SILLY. She couldn't remember the last time she wore a dress, much less one that was so long, and floofy, and, well... elegant.

Lizzy Bennet was not elegant. As evidenced by the scuffed black Converse hidden under the length and layers of the dress. She didn't particularly care if anyone noticed, but it might give her away if she bumped into Kitty and Lydia.

"You ready?" Beside her, Jane, dressed as Princess Peach, practically glowed in her flowing pink dress, her hair lightly curled, and her tiara perfectly placed. Her embroidered, pale pink mask didn't do a thing to hide her innate beauty.

Lizzy unconsciously played with the bracelet around her wrist. "As I'll ever be."

"Okay. I'll meet you back here at nine forty-five. They're going to announce homecoming king and queen then, so I doubt anyone will notice us leave."

"Sounds good. Just in case..." Lizzy pulled out her phone, opened her clock app to set an alarm for a quarter to ten. Then she slipped the phone back in the pocket of her dress, glanced at her best friend with a cheeky grin. "Let's go give 'em the ol' razzle-dazzle."

Chuckling, the two friends rounded the corner and stepped into the gymnasium.

The normally bland space was decked out with rows of gold fabric curtains, interspersed with trails of white ribbon and endless trickles of string lights, effectively covering the walls and closed bleachers. Some of the fabric and lights twisted and stretched toward the center of the ceiling, where a disco ball reflected all the twinkling lights and color. A dozen or so round tables were set up near a spread of refreshments, draped in white tablecloths and gauzy gold table runners, each with a centerpiece of white roses in a gold vase. A DJ oversaw the room from their spot on the stage at the far end, pumping musical ebb and flow into the crowd.

From her place moping at a table, Caroline sat surveying the crowd for Will. Her brother had told her Will wasn't going to wear the costume she'd picked out for him, but she'd been so sure he would. Now she sat alone while her friends danced, a Barbie without her Ken, finally wondering if Will had meant it when he said he wouldn't ask her out.

She'd seen the two princesses enter, and even she had to admit their ensemble was very good. They seemed unaware they'd drawn the eyes of the room. *Enjoy it while it lasts*, she thought, jealousy straightening her spine. *I'm still queen around here.*

From his spot near the concessions, Will happened to glance toward the gym entrance, and the latecomers caught his eye. As they drew closer into the room, walking down the gold carpet toward the dance floor, he paused, a cup of punch halfway to his lips.

His first thought was their costumes were clichéd—they were clearly Sleeping Beauty and Cinderella, yet high school was a little old to dress as a princess, wasn't it?

Then he had to acknowledge that was hypocritical of him. He was dressed as Prince Charming after all.

And as they walked further into the room, and he looked at them more closely, he had to admit they both looked amazing.

But it was Cinderella who caught his eye.

Lithe and lean, the vibrant, shimmering blue ballgown she wore swished around her legs like air, giving her the appearance of floating. Her mask, white and lacy, stood out against her auburn curls, which were piled high on her head, a few tendrils loose here and there.

He started to pull his eyes away—he didn't need a distraction right now—when Cinderella broke off from her friend.

And headed right for the disco ball.

Lizzy could admit to herself—barely—that she was nervous. Closet Poet could be literally anyone. What if they didn't like each other in person? What if he didn't show? It could all have been a joke. She could have been catfished!

At least the mask would keep any would-be jokers from realizing who she really was.

Even as she thought it, she heard a voice behind her that sent her nerves skittering like small droplets of ice.

"I see you've chosen to await a suitor directly under the ball of mirrors."

The ice on her skin left nothing but the chill of disappointment. She turned to face the speaker, thinking she should have known he would have been capable of recognizing her.

"Colin."

He was dressed as Matt Smith's eleventh Doctor, bowtie, fez, and all; and though she could admit he pulled the look off reasonably well, he ruined it with his somewhat leering smile.

"How delightful we should meet here," he said, and she cringed at his terrible impression of an English accent. "It seems time and relative dimension in space have brought us together on this special evening."

"The TARDIS does have a mind of its own," she quipped, and as if on cue, the music changed to something fast and pulsing.

"Indeed!" Without warning, he gripped her hands. "Do you not feel the urge to dance a reel?"

In fact, she did not. And why was he speaking like a Georgian gentleman? But she didn't have much of a chance to protest before he began swinging her around. She would have pulled back, but if he let go of her wrists in the midst of spinning, they'd both likely careen to the floor.

Thankfully, he soon slowed and let go—though it still threw her off balance a little—but this was followed up by his doing a sort of mock Irish jig in a circle around her.

What in the world?

She had to think of some way out of this. Anything.

She whipped her eyes around the room, and they landed on the refreshment table. Perfect!

"Excuse me," she said, trying to step around Colin. "I'm going to get some punch."

"Oh, allow me!" he insisted, gesturing with his hands for her to stay and rushing off.

She huffed at his back, the ice in her skin warming under the spark of her annoyance and dismay. He hadn't said he was Closet Poet, but he specifically mentioned the disco ball. Why would he say that if he wasn't? Unless someone else had told him to say that.

"I knew this was a catfish," she muttered.

"Lit Fairy?"

She froze.

This voice was warm, like honey in tea; hope sprang eternal as it heated and soothed her. And there was something familiar about it, but she couldn't place it.

This time when she turned, she allowed herself a small smile.

She had to look a up a little—he was tall. He wore slim, dark green pants and a stylish jacket reminiscent of royalty, with golden trim, buttons, and those pad things on the shoulder, tassels swinging lightly with his movement. His waistcoat was a dull gold color to match the trimming, and he even completed the look with a high-necked shirt and cravat.

His mask matched his suit, the green making his eyes pop in an almost ethereal way. And his hair was hidden under one of those fake white powdered wigs.

A bit of a disappointment, as it hid his identity a little too well. "Closet Poet?"

Relief swamped her when he smiled. His perception preceded him when he said, "You sound relieved."

"Let's just say I was a little worried there for a sec."

He glanced behind her, but she didn't dare turn around. "Do you want to get out of here?" he talk-shouted, as pounding music started to drown out their voices.

When she raised a brow, he grinned, and leaned toward her so he could speak close to her ear. "I meant to the courtyard. Fresh air, less bodies, more quiet. We'd actually be able to hear each other talk."

"That sounds perfect, actually," she agreed.

"Shall we?" He held out his elbow to her. Charmed, she took it and he led her away from the crowd.

Near the stage, cheering wildly for the DJ, were Kitty and Lydia; Lydia, dressed in a plastic yellow mini dress and yellow go-go boots, didn't notice when her yellow beret fell off her head. Kitty, in red bell bottoms, red go-go boots, and a red tank with matching feather boa, bent to pick it up. From their spot, she happened to glance toward the courtyard doors. Pausing, Kitty squinted at the couple heading outside.

"That girl looks familiar," she remarked.

Lydia only laughed as she took back her hat, and turned back to the DJ. Kitty shrugged and did the same.

While the twins battled for the DJ's attention, Elizabeth's breath hitched as she and Closet Poet entered the courtyard—she'd never seen it at night. The lights strung around the branches and trunks of the trees were glowing softly, giving the flowers a misty vibrance. She could hear the low babble of the fountain in the corner of the garden under the rustle of leaves in the breeze.

It was almost as if it were a different place; it didn't feel like the school.

She let go of his arm to wander the paths a bit, and he followed, fingers laced behind his back, watching her.

"So," he prompted.

"So."

After a few beats of silence she glanced at him. "Don't tell me you're better at talking online than in person."

"Maybe I am." He shrugged. "At least, I'm often more comfortable with messaging, as it gives me more time to think about my reply."

"I get that. After talking with you so much, I got the sense you're a very introspective person."

"Some would say too much. That I'm too reserved."

"Do you think you are?"

The question caught him off guard, but he rallied quickly. "Yes."

She tiled her head. "And you think it's a bad thing?"

"Perhaps sometimes," he admitted after a moment. "Mostly, it is what it is. But there are times when I wish I had the conviction to speak up."

She knew he was likely speaking of his father, an angsty subject for him, so she endeavored to change it.

"Who do you think will win homecoming king and queen?"

He made a *pfft* noise and shook his head. "No idea. And I don't care. Why? Who'd you vote for?"

"Oh, I didn't vote at all," she grinned, a little mischievously if he was on the mark. "And it sounds like you didn't either."

"Never even considered it, though my friends would be shocked to hear it."

"So you're the kind of guy expected to go along with convention, but in your own quiet way you're fighting against it."

It was an admirable way to put it, even if it didn't feel entirely accurate to him. "I'm trying to."

"Is that why you're dressed like a prince charming, then?" Her lips curved as she tipped up her chin. "And does it fit convention, or is it a small act of rebellion?"

"Perhaps a bit of both," he said, thinking of how he'd finally told Caroline to back off. When she raised a brow, which he took as a request for further information, he shook his head. "And what about you? Isn't Cinderella a bit conventional? A classic romantic fairytale?"

"Depends on the version of the story," she said airily.

"I guess I was thinking of the Disney movie. That Cinderella was just as hyped about meeting the prince as all the other girls."

A defensive frown twisted her mouth. "Hey, that Cinderella did *not* go to the ball to meet the prince. She just wanted to go and have a good time—she didn't even know it was the prince she was dancing with until the next day."

"Huh. I never noticed that." It certainly added a new angle to the story. "That version of her still seems a little...useless to me, I guess. Maybe I'll have to rewatch it with this new perspective."

"My dad loved Cinderella," she said quietly. "He always used to say her kindness was her strength. And the more I come across different versions of her, the more I find I also appreciate her patience and her resilience. Even her courage. She makes the best she can of a bad situation until she's able to defy her stepmother."

It sounded deeper, more personal than the words themselves implied. "Is that what you try to do with your stepmother?"

"Key word: Try. I fully admit I'm defying her by being here tonight, with the help of some friends."

"So this Cinderella actually *is* hyped to meet the prince," he teased.

She pursed her lips in a pout, but still couldn't hide the smile underneath it. "I suppose, in this case. But, anyway, since you were so keen to mention a useless damsel, I think it only fair to mention a useless hunk."

"Okay." He sputtered out a laugh. "Go right ahead."

"I've heard people say Eric is the most useless Disney prince, but that's total crap." She gestured with her hands, as if to emphasize the injustice. "If anything, he's one of the most useful—he actively fights Ursula, and is the one who kills her, with a sunken ship, no less. That's ingenuity."

"So who is the most useless Disney prince, then?"

"Ironically, probably Cinderella's prince charming."

Bemused, he cocked his head. "Why do you say that?"

"Because he doesn't do anything." She said it like it was obvious. "He's forced to attend the ball by his father, dances with Cinderella at the ball, and that's it—he doesn't even do the shoe thing. It's the Duke that goes around with the glass slipper, at the command of the king."

"He has an actual character arc in the live action remake."

She gave him a saucy look, not at all phased he'd just admitted to seeing it. "Touché, but the live action remakes are a whole other kettle. We're talking animated Disney films here."

"Fair enough," he allowed. There was something about the way she said it that struck him. As he thought again of the spark in her eyes, the snark in her tone, pieces started fitting together.

Well, he supposed. The best way to figure her out would be to keep her talking.

"I can tell from your arguments that *The Little Mermaid* is a favorite of yours, but what about least favorites?"

"Hm." She pressed her lips together for a moment. "Well, there are a few I feel differently about now than I did when I was younger. But I remember disliking *The Hunchback of Notre Dame* when I was a kid."

He noted she used the correct pronunciation of Notre Dame, tucked it away as a clue to her identity. "Why is that? I always thought it was cool."

She squinted at him. "I bet you had a crush on Esmerelda."

"Duh. She's hot, and a total badass," he pointed out, hesitating before continuing, "And genuinely kind underneath it all."

She seemed taken aback at this last part, pausing to consider him. "I liked her, too," she admitted. "But Frodo scared me as a kid."

"Frollo," he corrected, enjoying her. "Frodo is from *Lord of the Rings*."

"Right."

He smirked at her. "Have you not seen *Lord of the Rings?*"

"I have, it's just...you know—a lot to sit through."

"It is," he agreed. "But it's an epic marathon. Nine-plus hours of magic and adventure."

She gave him a blank stare. "One does not simply binge watch such lengthy tomes."

He laughed. "I understand what you mean, but it's not impossible."

"Anyway," she continued, smiling. "*Frollo* doesn't scare me anymore; now I just think he's a disgusting, horrible, self-righteous creep."

"That...is accurate."

She frowned a little. "Sorry, I just made the conversation a little morbid. Pick a happy topic."

"How about we play twenty questions? Get to know each other on a more basic level now that we've met in person?"

"Twenty seems like a lot. How about ten?"

"Ten it is. What's your...favorite food?"

"Ice cream."

"Mine's pizza."

"Of course," she said, and he could hear the eye roll in her tone. Then she straightened, another mischievous smile taking over her face. In a deliberately low pitched, gravely voice she said, "What...is your favorite color?"

A laugh burst out of him. "What, you're not going to ask me the air speed velocity of an unladen swallow? Blue, I guess."

"You guess?"

He shrugged. "There's too many colors to have a true favorite. What about you?"

"Green. But, like, forest green and sage green; not in your face, like lime green, you know?"

"So, dark and muted greens, got it." She nodded and he took a few moments to consider his next question. Maybe it was time to get a little bit deeper. "Okay. Favorite book?"

"Ooh, going there, are we?"

"We've talked about books before."

"We have, but not our favorites." Then she affected a serious expression. "It's a tie between *The Hunchback of Notre Dame* and *The Fellowship of the Ring*."

When he chuckled, she grinned, then sighed. "No, nothing against Victor Hugo or Tolkien, but I don't think I can choose a favorite. I've got my favorites I like to re-read, my favorite series, my favorite reading experiences—like, books that I'll probably never read again, but I remember fondly because it gave me a good cry or something."

"I'm glad you feel that way," he confessed. "What I said about colors? It applies to books, too."

"Agreed."

The thought that he knew her niggled at him. She was funny, she could quote Monty Python, and she could debate her opinion with passion, be it books or Disney movies. Who did he know with auburn hair and blue eyes that had such a fiery wit?

As their walk around the courtyard took them back toward the doors to the gym, music filtered out, the high energy tones switching to softer, slower ones. Grinning, he paused, held out a hand to her.

"Shall we dance, my lady?"

He was surprised when she bit her lip. "No one's ever asked me to dance before," she admitted quietly, taking his hand.

"Weren't you just dancing with that other guy?"

She sighed, placing her hand on his shoulder as he stepped into her, laid a hand on her lower back. "He didn't ask, he just... swung me around," she said as he began to lead them in slow circles.

He thought of the way the moron had been dancing around her before he'd approached.

"Any guy who doesn't treat you right is an idiot."

She shrugged. "He's harmless. He's got a crush on me, and I should probably tell him I don't feel that way about him. But I don't want to hurt his feelings, so I just avoid him as much as possible, and politely accept his attention when I can't."

He frowned. "That's stupid. His feelings aren't your responsibility. If he's bothering you, you should tell him to back off."

"I know. I actually kind of hope he'll finally ask me out so I have a reason to give a firm no."

He didn't like the idea of that at all, and his hand flexed on her waist.

"What if you...had a boyfriend?"

Her eyes whipped up to his. "Then I suppose I wouldn't have to reject him."

She looked at him so intently he could feel a blush covering his own face. He swallowed, looking down to give himself a moment to recover.

And there, unmistakably, was a pair of faded black Chucks peeking out from under her dress. With this final piece, the image came together.

There was no doubt in his mind he was looking at Elizabeth Bennet.

Shock struck him dumb for several moments. Lizzy Bennet—the intrepid Elizabeth—was Lit Fairy, the girl he'd been longing to meet. The girl he'd spent the past several months opening up to, talking to like he had to no one else.

Falling for.

Once he got over the shock, he surprised himself by realizing he wasn't disappointed in the slightest.

There'd always been...*something* between him and Lizzy. A simmer under the surface of their teasing. Sure, she sometimes got under his skin—but he'd often come away from their interactions smiling. They liked to rile each other up.

But now he knew they could really talk to each other, too. She was wicked smart, and witty, which were things he'd always appreciated about her; but now he could recognize he was drawn to her for those reasons. A lot of girls bored him, but she never had.

She was pretty, of course, but Elizabeth had never used that to her advantage, another thing he appreciated about her. She didn't even wear makeup.

Except tonight. The lids of her velvet blue eyes—he understood now it was too dark to see the violent tint to them—were colored with some sparkly, smokey eyeshadow, popping against the black of her eyeliner and the white of her mask. And her smirking lips were brushed with a dark pink.

He had to swallow the urge to kiss her. A new sensation where Lizzy Bennet was concerned.

He hoped she wasn't put off by his silence; hopefully she thought he was just too caught up in their dance to say anything.

Should he tell her he knew who she was? Should he reveal himself? Chances were she was wondering the same thing herself.

"Next question," he prompted.

She tilted her head back to look up at him, her gaze now assessing, her voice quieter. "I know you implied it, but I want to be clear. Do you want to see me again?"

"One hundred percent." His heart pounded as he smiled, and her answering smile had him drawing her closer. "Do you want to see me?"

"Hm." She tipped her face, pursed her lips as she pretended to think about it. "I suppose there's room in my schedule for you."

When her eyes met his he realized he'd been staring, mesmerized. Slowly, he lifted a hand to cradle her cheek, leaned his head down. Her eyes widened, but she didn't back away, instead tilting her face up.

So he did what he'd been wanting to, and pressed his lips to hers. When he felt hers pressing back, he cupped her face and deepened the kiss a little, allowing the sizzle between them to grow before pulling away.

Her eyes blinked open, pert mouth poised to speak when bright, ringing bell tones sounded loud and clear.

"Crap." She reached into the pocket of her dress, pulled out her phone, turning off the alarm. "I have to go."

"What, why?"

"Curfew." She started gathering up the voluminous skirt. "If I don't get back in time, I'm dead."

"Okay, well—"

"I'm sorry," she said, and took off, skirts floating behind her.

He only hesitated a few seconds before he went after her.

Five

SHE FELT bad for leaving Closet Poet behind, but there wasn't time now. They could arrange to meet up again later. She'd message him as soon as she got home.

Right now, getting back to the café before Frances was most important. Which meant she needed to find Jane pronto.

She ran back into the gym, zigzagged her way through dancing couples, eyes alert for her friend. She thought perhaps Jane would be among them—Jane attracted attention wherever she went, so someone had likely asked her to dance.

She moved toward the refreshment table in an effort to get a better view of the room, her eyes drifting over a couple locked in a passionate embrace against the curtains where the folded up bleachers were.

Wait. Was that...?

"Jane?"

Indeed it was Jane, her lips glued to those of an elfin boy in a green cap—likely Link. She was happy for her friend, but once again, there was no time.

"Jane!" she said, louder this time, as the student body president was getting ready to announce who'd been voted homecoming king and queen, and rushed over to the kissing couple. "We have to go right now."

Jane pried her lips away from Link's, her eyes a little dazed under the hearts in them. "Oh," she said softly, then looked at Link—and Lizzy could tell even through his green mask it was none other than Charlie Bingley. "I'm sorry, I have to take my friend home."

"I understand, my lady." Charlie offered her a smile and raised her hand to his lips. "Until we meet again."

Elizabeth could see Jane was about to melt where she stood, so she gripped her friend's arm and began tugging her away.

"She'll see you on Monday," she told Charlie, then pulled Jane through the crowd. Jane seemed to come to her senses, pushing ahead and rushing toward the exit.

Behind her, she heard, "Your king and queen are Will Darcy and Caroline Bingley!" Mentally rolling her eyes at the whoops and cheers, she nearly tripped over her skirts, flinging her arms out to balance herself before picking them up and passing up Jane as they ran through the doors, into the hall.

She was fast, Will thought as he tried to follow—it probably helped that she was wearing sneakers instead of heels. He lost sight of her for several moments, weaving his way through the crowd toward the other side of the gym; if she was leaving, she'd be heading for the exit.

He finally caught sight of her near the bleachers, tugging her friend, who he now realized was Jane Benson, away from...Charlie?

He'd question his friend later, he thought, pivoting to follow Elizabeth. He didn't pay any attention to what was going on in the gym until he heard his name announced from the stage, along with Caroline's.

He paused when he saw Elizabeth nearly trip, spreading her

arms—and the bracelet she'd been wearing flying off her wrist. He scrambled to catch up to her, but she didn't notice the bracelet, instead lifting her skirts and picking up her pace.

He sidetracked to pick up the bracelet, but when he rose, glanced at the door, she was gone.

"Will Darcy? Are you here?"

He whipped around, noting Caroline had taken the stage and was already wearing her crown, beaming out at the crowd. Confusion was evident on their faces as everyone began glancing around, looking for him.

He looked down at the dainty bracelet in his hands—little gold roses with tiny pearls in between—debating whether he wanted to accept the crown.

He certainly didn't want to stand next to Caroline. Or pretend to be happy for winning something he didn't care about. For once, he didn't feel the need to cave to the pressure.

That decided it, he supposed, tucking the bracelet in his pocket. He'd find Charlie, head home, and figure out what to say to Elizabeth.

Should he wait until Monday? Or should he message her, let her know he had the bracelet?

"Dude," Charlie said, approaching him and gesturing to the stage. "You gonna go up there?"

"Nah."

"Okay." Charlie just nodded, like the friend he was. "Wanna head out?"

"Sure—I've got quite a story to tell you."

"So do I." Charlie beamed.

Will clapped his friend on the back as they left the gym. "I bet you do."

Lizzy practically dove into Jane's car. "Step on it!"

"I'll go as fast as the speed limit allows," Jane assured her. "Frances hasn't even arrived to pick up the girls yet, so we should be fine."

As if on cue, a familiar car pulled into the lot, making the hairs on the back of Lizzy's neck stand up. "Crap!" she said, ducking forward so no one could see her through the window.

Jane carefully pulled past Frances' car, which had stopped in the drop off zone with other waiting parents, but she needn't have worried—the woman was fixing her makeup in the mirror and didn't bother to glance in their direction.

"You're clear," she told Lizzy as she pulled out onto the road.

"Okay." Lizzy blew out a breath. "Now seriously, can you push the speed limit a little, just this once?"

"I'll do my best."

Lizzy nodded, then slowly grinned as she removed her mask. "So. Charlie Bingley, huh?"

"Oh my God," Jane squealed. "I totally kissed Charlie Bingley!"

Lizzy felt giddy herself. "And I totally kissed...Closet Poet." Her smile faded as she remembered she hadn't discovered who he was.

"You don't know who he is?"

"No, and he doesn't know who I am, either. We agreed we wanted to see each other again, he kissed me, and then my alarm when off and I ran."

"Lizzy!"

"What? I panicked. And I can message him later."

Jane didn't respond, but her disapproving frown said it all.

Ignoring her, Elizabeth turned and reached into the back, pulling her messenger bag from the back seat. She dug in the front pocket, pulled out a packet of makeup wipes, and began scrubbing hastily at her face as she flipped open the mirror on the visor.

She had a clump of wipes when she was finished, and shoved them back in the pocket.

It was then she noticed her wrist was bare. She stilled.

"Oh no," she whispered through hitched breath. Scrambling, she bent forward again, scoured the car floor with her hands.

"What?" Jane was worried enough to take her eyes off the road for a moment and glance at her.

"My mom's bracelet." Tears pressed against the back of her eyes as she ruffled the folds of her skirt, already feeling it was hopeless. "It fell off."

She gave the car another cursory glance before giving up, pinching the bridge of her nose to keep herself from crying. "I must have lost it at the dance."

"Do you want to go back?"

"No, it's too late. I can't risk running into Frances or the twins, and there's no time." She huffed, more out of defeat than frustration. "Besides, there's no way I'd find it in that crowd. It's gone."

"I'm sorry." Jane sounded just as defeated as she felt.

"Me, too." But she couldn't think about it now. She was still wearing the dress, and she didn't want to risk bringing it into the café. So she snatched up her bag, tossed it into the back seat, and unbuckled her seatbelt.

Jane's eyes widened. "What are you doing?"

"I have to change," Lizzy said before Jane could scold her, turning to wedge herself between the seats and climb into the back. She twisted her body, finally plopping onto the cramped seat before opening her bag. She unzipped the dress, carefully pushed the top half down to her waist before pulling her t-shirt over her head.

Then she lifted her hips as she shimmied out of the rest of the dress. It took some maneuvering, but she finally got her jeans on. She let out a breath when she realized they were only a couple minutes away from the café now.

Carefully, she folded the dress, debating whether or not to stuff it in her bag. But on the off chance someone would see it and realize she'd been at the dance, she decided she should return it to Charlotte. As Jane pulled into the café's parking lot, she laid the folded dress on the seat beside her, gave it one last caress for good measure.

"Thanks, Mom," she whispered.

When Jane parked, she pushed the front seat forward and leapt out of the car. She likely had a few minutes at least, but her nerves wanted her safely ensconced behind the counter before Frances returned.

"Thank you, Jane. Talk later?"

"Absolutely. What about the dress?"

"I'll get it back to Charlotte. Can you hold onto it for now? The mask, too?"

Jane nodded. "You better get inside. *Cinderella*." When she winked, Lizzy rolled her eyes, closed the passenger door. She waved as she jogged to the café door, then rushed inside.

She could see Charlotte relax visibly when she saw her.

"You had me worried, there," she said, though she smiled as Lizzy rounded the counter. "How was the dance?"

She was really asking how meeting Closet Poet had gone, Lizzy knew, and delayed responding by making a beeline for the kitchen. She could feel Charlotte's eyes on her, as well as Mary's, Maddie's, and Ed's, but she focused on taking her apron from its hook, hanging up her bag.

She finally turned to them as she slipped the apron on, began tying it.

"It was...really nice," she said honestly.

"You mean he was nice?" Maddie probed.

"He was. He was a real prince charming."

"So you're going to see him again, right?" Ed asked.

Here she faltered, shrugging sheepishly.

"We agreed we want to see each other again, but we never revealed our identities before I ran out of time. It's okay," she held up her hands when she saw their faces. "I can text him later."

"You could text him now," Mary pointed out.

"I could," she admitted as she tied her hair into a hasty bun. Sighing, she pulled her phone from the other front pocket of her bag. As she opened her messages, the bell over the café door jingled, followed by an almost immediate shout.

"Where is Elizabeth?!"

Lizzy cursed, shoving her phone back in her bag, then running over to the supply shelf.

"If that ungrateful girl went to that dance..." Frances was saying as she neared the kitchen.

"She's back here," Charlotte said, just as Lizzy's eyes landed on a box of napkins. She snatched it up in time for Frances to appear in the kitchen doorway, hands on the hips of her skin-tight hot pink pants. She looked like Barbie's mom, having paired the pants with a pale blue blouse with a pink floral pattern.

"What are you doing? Why is no one up front?"

"Just going to restock the napkins at the tables," Lizzy said, holding up the box as she walked over to the kitchen door. Frances narrowed her eyes, as if looking for signs of deception in her appearance or demeanor—but maybe that was her nerves talking.

Finally, Frances sniffed and stepped back. "Fine. But make the girls their smoothies first."

"Sure," Lizzy said, eyes shifting to where Kitty and Lydia stood on the other side of the counter. She had to bite back a smile when she saw their costumes; they both actually looked great, but it wasn't until she saw the bright yellow and red outfits she realized they must have gone with Lydia's 'sexy ketchup and mustard' idea. The interpretation was certainly interesting.

"How was the dance?"

"O.M.G. it was *so* epic," Lydia gushed. "All the guys wanted to dance with me, and the DJ was, like, totally hitting on me."

"He was not!" Kitty insisted. "He totally ignored you."

"No, he was ignoring *you*."

To distract herself from making some sarcastic remark, Lizzy set about making their smoothies—green for Lydia, peanut butter and banana for Kitty.

"Oh, yeah, and of course Will Darcy and Caroline Bingley were king and queen," Lydia continued. "But, like, Will didn't go up to accept his crown."

"Really?" Normally, Lizzy didn't engage with Kitty and Lydia's gossiping, but in this case curiosity won out. She had a hard time believing school golden boy Darcy wouldn't do his popularity duty; but then again, she'd witnessed him basically telling Caroline to stop harassing him only a few hours before. She couldn't blame him if he didn't want to stand next to her like they were together, or dance the king and queen dance with her.

"Yeah!" Kitty bounced on her toes. "Caroline just stood up there by herself, and—"

"I'm telling the story!" Lydia cut in. "So anyway, no one knew what Will was dressed as. Since Caroline was Barbie, we all assumed he'd be Ken, but Ricky Fitzwilliam was actually dressed as Ken, and he danced the king and queen dance with her."

Lydia preened as though she'd just delivered some extremely important news. Watching her to make sure she was done before speaking, Kitty added, "No one knows who said it, but after that it was all over the dance that Caroline came to the dance without a date. Will never asked her.”

Her thunder stolen, Lydia pouted, but Lizzy headed off a tantrum by handing her her smoothie. She didn’t add she already knew this news, as the twins would grill her for information, and as much as she disliked the people in question, she refused to gossip about them.

“Sounds eventful,” was all she said.

“I wonder why he didn’t ask her,” Kitty said aloud.

“O.M.G. who cares?” Lydia scoffed. “What matters is Will Darcy is for sure single, which means I totally have a shot with him.”

Now Kitty scoffed. “As if. If anything he’d want me, because I’m older.”

“By fourteen minutes! Besides, I’m way more fun!”

“Are not!”

“Girls!” Frances finally cut in. “I’m sure this young man would like a chance with either one of you. Though you have to admit, Kitty dear, that Lydia is more lively, and a bit prettier.”

Lizzy highly doubted that, but she’d leave them to their delusions. She finished up Kitty’s smoothie, held it out to her, but Kitty was looking at her sister and mother with something resembling hurt.

“Now come along girls,” Frances was saying. “I’ve got a busy day tomorrow.”

She sauntered toward the door, Lydia flouncing behind her. Kitty finally noticed the smoothie in Lizzy’s hand.

“Thanks, Lizzy,” she said, taking it.

Lizzy warred with herself, sighed.

“Kitty,” she called, and Kitty paused at the door. “You’re just as fun and pretty as Lydia.”

For a moment—just a moment—Kitty’s face softened into a

grateful smile. Then Frances hollered Kitty's name from outside and the brief connection was lost. Kitty visibly straightened herself.

"Whatever," she said, and walked out the door.

So much for trying, Lizzy thought. Perhaps it was best to remember that some people never changed.

Six

SOMETHING WAS DIFFERENT, Lizzy thought. There was an undercurrent in the halls as she walked to her locker on Monday morning, but it was hard to pinpoint what it was. She thought maybe the school was abuzz with news of the dance—namely Will's absence—and Will's rejection of Caroline; but as she glanced around at the faces of all the guys she passed by, she wondered if *she* was different.

Knowing Closet Poet went to the same school was one thing, but meeting him, talking to him face to face, seeing he was real—somehow that made being at school feel different. He was here. She just didn't know who he was, which was probably why she unconsciously examined the face of every guy she saw, looking for him.

He'd messaged her on Sunday, something she had originally planned to do as well. But she had yet to respond, which had prompted another text from him that morning.

CLOSET POET

We agreed to see each other again, did we not?

It stung her heart. She wanted to see him again, to look into those bright green eyes without a mask, and—her heart pounded to think of it—to kiss him again.

But with time to consider it all, her doubts had returned. What if he was disappointed when he found out who she was? Or even if he wasn't, how would they make it work with Frances interfering in her life, or when they went off to different colleges?

It didn't help that Frances watched her with suspicion all day Sunday, as if looking for an excuse to punish her. Lizzy was afraid Frances would pounce if she looked at her phone too much. Her one consolation was seeing the deformed lobster pink smiley face on Frances's back, in the spots where she had "missed" putting sunscreen, as she helped Frances with her morning routine.

She would explain this to Closet Poet at some point. Soon. She wouldn't ghost him—and she knew it was unfair to delay her reply. Maybe Jane could help her during lunch.

"Did you message Closet Poet yet?" Jane asked, in echo of her thoughts.

Lizzy winced. "No. I was just thinking about what to say to him. I know I need to reply soon."

They reached their lockers, went about their morning routine.

"What about you?" Lizzy asked, pulling out a textbook. "Are you going to say anything to Charlie?"

Predictably, Jane blushed. "I don't know. He's probably forgotten all about it by now."

"Jane. No one could forget you." Giving her friend an assuring look, Lizzy closed her locker, and turning, nearly knocked right into Colin.

"Gah!" Hand over her speeding heart, she was flustered enough to snap, "You've got to stop doing that!"

"Good morning, Elizabeth." He smiled at her as though she

hadn't just scolded him, and seemed even more excitable than usual.

"Good morning, Colin," she said warily, starting to move around him. "I have to get to class."

"This will only take a moment!" He held out an arm to stop her, then slanted a significant look at Jane before looking back at her very directly. "I was hoping to speak to you privately."

"Oh. Jane and I have no secrets. Anything you have to say, you can say in front of her."

"But—"

"It's okay," Jane cut in, giving Lizzy an apologetic look. "I have to use the restroom. I'll see you in class, Lizzy."

"Jane!"

But Jane scurried off to the girls' bathroom, and while Lizzy was distracted looking after her, Colin took her hand.

"I'm sure my attentions to you have not gone unnoticed, Elizabeth."

Inwardly, Lizzy cringed. Just a few days ago, she'd told Closet Poet she wanted a reason to put Colin's attentions off of her, and now it seemed like she was about to get her wish.

Be careful what you wish for, she thought, drawing her hand out of his and gripping the strap of her bag.

He barely noticed, instead giving her a leering smile as he continued, "I admit I was unsure at first if I wanted to unite myself with someone as low on the social totem pole as you, but I realized you have other, much better qualities that make up for that lack."

She noted how he ran his eyes down her body, narrowed her own back at him. "Excuse you?"

"And now, let me assure you I will no longer toy with your delicate emotions. Shall I tell you what I have planned for our first date?" He tipped his head to ogle her, and she didn't bother hiding her anger or her grimace.

He hadn't asked her on a date, but regardless he expected her to go on one with him. She reached down—deep, deep down—for some patience before she responded.

"No, thank you. I'm sorry, but I don't want to go on a date with you."

He blinked. "There's no need to play hard to get, Elizabeth. I've set my objection to you aside, and not being single might raise your social status a bit."

Lizzy's jaw worked as she sent him a bland stare. "I'm not playing anything. I am single by *choice*, and I am *choosing* to keep it that way. Thank you for asking me out, but I'm not interested."

Now he frowned at her, something she had yet to see from him, and straightened to peer at her out of narrowed eyes. "You do realize you're not likely to get a better offer, right?"

Something between a scoff and a snort escaped Lizzy's mouth. "Did you just suggest no one will ever ask me out again, like, for the rest of my life? You do realize this is high school, right?" she mocked his previous tone.

"Of course, but our high school years are the stepping stones of our lives. Even if we only date for a little while, your having gone out with me will make you more desirable to other men. Therefore, I can only think you're just being coy and will ultimately accept me."

"If nothing I've said so far has convinced you I'm serious, I'm not sure what will." Adjusting her bag on her shoulder, Lizzy glared at him. "The answer is *no*, Colin. Now, I really have to get to class."

She stepped around him, but he called after her. "So this is the thanks I get for giving you my attentions!"

The halls were mercifully empty, as the bell would ring in another minute—thankfully, her first class was around the corner. She paused to turn back and deliver a parting blow.

"Nobody asked you to pay attention to me, Colin. You did that of your own free will, without any encouragement from me. And as you've just learned, paying attention to a girl is never a guarantee of acceptance."

Pivoting, she quickened her pace, ignoring his protests. She managed to make it to her desk seconds before the bell rang.

"So, did you hear from her?"

Charlie's eager smile only had Will frowning more than he already was. "No."

After the dance, Charlie had explained how his evening had gone, a dreamy expression taking over his features when he mentioned Jane. Will had then recounted his history with Lit Fairy, including his secret identity, and told his friend of his discovery; Charlie had been surprised but supportive, and excited, since Lizzy was Jane's best friend. Will had also reached out to Lizzy over the weekend, and that morning, but she still hadn't responded to either message. He knew she probably had her reasons, but it was still discouraging.

He'd debated with himself multiple times about whether to tell her he knew who she was—and whether or not he should reveal himself. But it seemed she wasn't ready, and he didn't want to just blurt it out. Though, there was also the matter of her bracelet to consider. She probably thought she'd lost it, and he wanted to restore it to her. Even now, its presence in the front pocket of his backpack felt like it was burning a hole.

"Oh." Charlie's smile fell briefly before lighting up again. "Well, we're about to see her and Jane at lunch. Do you think I should tell her it was me? Do you think she likes me?"

Will wasn't totally sure Charlie's excitement was warranted.

Jane was perfectly nice, and certainly very pretty, but he'd never seen her stare longingly at Charlie the way he did her.

"I'm not sure."

"Oh, hey!" Charlie thwacked him in the shoulder as they walked. "You should tell Lizzy it was you."

If only it were that easy. "I'm not sure about that either."

"Oh, c'mon, it's not like she'd be disappointed. You're Will Darcy."

Was he afraid she'd be disappointed? Charlie wasn't wrong—pretty much every girl at school would kill or maim to be his girlfriend. He usually preferred being single, but he wouldn't be for long if he could help it.

Lizzy was different, though. She was just as hard to read as Jane. Maybe he had every reason to be nervous as Charlie. She did call him 'jerkwad' sometimes—either she was hiding her feelings behind a veneer of snark, or she meant it.

He hoped it was the former.

"Tell you what." He clapped Charlie's shoulder as they entered the courtyard, saw the subjects of their affection already sitting at their usual table. "If you tell Jane it was you, then I'll tell Lizzy it was me."

"Deal."

Much of the lunch crowd had yet to pile in, so it was quieter as they approached Lizzy and Jane's table, and they were able to pick up a snippet of their conversation.

"His costume did a really good job of hiding his identity," Lizzy was saying. "The main thing I noticed was how green his eyes were, even in the dim lighting."

"Hm." Jane tilted her head. "Will Darcy has green eyes. And he's in AP Lit with you, right? He probably knows a thing or two about poetry."

"*Darcy?* Ha!" Will wondered at the scoff in Lizzy's voice.

"There's no way it's him. That jerkwad wouldn't know charm if it smacked him in the face."

Will halted; it took Charlie a moment, but he stopped, too, a question in his gaze.

"Well, you won't find out who he is until you text him back," Jane said.

"I know," Lizzy grumbled. "I just need to figure out how to handle...everything."

"Um." Will looked at Charlie, spoke under his breath. "You go ahead. I don't think now's the right time for me."

Charlie gave him a commiserating look, nodded. "Wish me luck."

Will had already started walking to their table, but glanced back over his shoulder. "Good luck."

Quite the wrench had just been thrown into his plans, Will thought. He didn't exactly know why, but he had a pretty good impression that Lizzy didn't like him.

Which wasn't necessarily a bad thing—the him she saw was the fake one, the him he didn't really like either. He'd worn his mask with her as he had everybody else, so he couldn't exactly blame her. But of course, she would be one of the few girls who wouldn't drool over him because of who he was. That made revealing himself to her a bit more complicated.

Although, if she were the type to drool over him just because he was Will Darcy, she wouldn't be the kind of girl he wanted. Oh, the irony.

But hope wasn't entirely lost. She liked Closet Poet, the side of him he'd never revealed to anyone but her. She'd kissed Closet Poet.

She'd kissed *him*.

The memory of her soft, pert lips moving under his was enough to inspire him to win her heart as himself. All he had to do was let her get to know the real Will Darcy, and prove to her that he and Closet Poet were indeed one and the same.

Lizzy watched Jane's eyes go wide, and turned to see Charlie Bingley step up to their table.

"Uh...hey." He shuffled a bit, stuck his hands in his pockets. "So, you might not recognize me, Princess Peach, but I was—"

"Link." Jane rose, and moved to stand in front of him. "I knew it was you."

"You did?"

She nodded. "But I'm surprised you knew it was me."

"I wouldn't have kissed you if I didn't know it was you." Like he had at the dance, he took her hand, pressed a light kiss to her fingers.

"I wouldn't have let you if I didn't know it was you."

They were both staring so deeply into each other's eyes, as adorable as a couple in a Rogers and Hammerstein film, Lizzy doubted they noticed anything around them. Feeling superfluous, she deliberately pulled her gaze away from the starry eyed couple and glanced around the courtyard. More people were filing in, so it might look weird if she just left their table to go stand in a corner.

But then her eyes landed on the Brat Pack table. Will was sitting alone, watching the scene between Jane and his friend with a furrowed brow and distinct frown.

Did he disapprove of everything?

As if he knew she was looking at him, his gaze shifted, met hers. He smirked, nodded at her. Before she could wonder what that was about, he cocked his head as if to beckon her over. When she frowned at him, he lifted a hand, waved her over.

She narrowed her eyes, but quietly stood and walked over to him, plopped onto the bench across from him.

"You beckoned, Your Highness?"

He lifted a brow at her sharp tone. "You looked like you needed a reason to excuse yourself from the situation," he said, nodding toward their friends.

She covered her surprise he'd discerned her feelings with snark. "So you invited me to hold court with you?"

He shrugged. "I imagine we'll be seeing a lot more of each other. Might as well get used to it."

"What do you mean?"

"Link and Sleeping Beauty over there. Unless she says no, they'll be dating; as their respective best friends, we'll likely spend at least a little time together. What?" he asked at her chuckle.

"She was Princess Peach, not Princess Aurora."

"Oh." His frown was back, but she stopped herself from commenting on it when she remembered what he'd said in class the other day about his thinking face. Though it added another layer of surprise, she had to consider that maybe he didn't disapprove like she'd thought. In fact, he seemed to accept Jane and Charlie dating as sure thing. "That makes sense. I guess I just thought..."

"You thought?" she pushed when he trailed off.

Slowly, his eyes met hers, held. In the back of her mind she had a moment to acknowledge Jane was right—his eyes were a vibrant green. Green and searching.

It's like he can see right into me, she thought, then felt silly for thinking it. And in the next moment she felt uncomfortable under that discerning gaze.

Just as she was about to look away, he said, "I thought she was Aurora because the friend she came with was dressed as Cinderella."

Since he was still looking right at her when he said it, there was no way he missed the sudden panic that overtook her face. Jane was friendly with everybody, but Lizzy was her only true friend, and therefore the only one whom Jane would show up at a dance with. Will wasn't stupid, so he'd obviously figured out for himself that Lizzy was Cinderella.

"Did I say something wrong?" He was frowning again, but it actually seemed like he was concerned.

"You can't tell anyone," she said.

"I can't tell anyone what?"

"That I was Cinderella," she whispered, then lowered her voice even more. "No one can find out I was at the dance at all."

"Okay, but why?"

She sighed. "Look, I know the lives of us plebs are no concern to you, but I was forbidden to attend the dance. If anyone found out I was there, it might get back to my stepsisters. And if it got back to my stepsisters, they would tell my stepmother. And if my stepmother found out, I'd be toast. Worse than that—I'd be burnt toast, slowly disintegrating into blackened, bitter crumbs."

A slow grin spread over his face, and her stomach did a weird little tumble—she told herself it was simply nerves, fear he would't keep her secret.

"Well aren't you quite the rebel?" he teased.

"I'm serious." She stared daggers at him, but he kept smiling, like he found her distress amusing.

"I know. I won't mention it to anyone, and neither will Charlie; don't worry, you will not be toasted on my watch."

She'd stop worrying when the dance and all the gossip surrounding it was well behind them. Maybe.

"What are you doing at our table?!"

They both turned at the screech to see Caroline storming up to them, the remainder of the Brat Pack close behind her. Before

Lizzy could come up with a scathing remark, Will said, "I needed to talk to Elizabeth about AP Lit."

Caroline balked, whatever response was on the tip of her tongue swallowed by pure shock. "You're in an AP class?" she asked Will.

"You didn't know that?" Lizzy couldn't help asking.

"I'm in several AP classes," Will confirmed. "I have been every year."

"But..." Caroline could only gape at him. This clearly did not fit her perception of him.

Lizzy stood to make room for Anne and Louisa as Ricky sat next to Will. It was only then Caroline realized her brother wasn't at the table, and used this to try to recover. "Where on earth is Charlie?"

Lizzy said nothing, thinking it would be better to stay out of the drama. She started heading back to her table, where Jane and Charlie were now sitting together, still oblivious to their surroundings.

But she heard Will answer, "He's sitting over there with Jane."

"WHAT?"

Lizzy was sure Caroline had whipped around and noticed the pair looking rather cozy when she hissed, "*What is he doing over there?* Will, go get him, now."

Will's scoff was laced with disbelief. But instead of pointing out she wasn't the boss of him or her brother, he said, "Actually, Elizabeth invited me to join them. Hold up, Elizabeth."

Lizzy stopped, though more out of astonishment than compliance. She turned to see Will slinging his backpack over his shoulder as he jogged to catch up to her.

"Will!" Caroline was still standing, trying to recover from yet another shock. The others only looked on in confusion.

"What are you doing?" Lizzy whispered to Will when he joined her.

This time the grin he gave her was absolutely mischievous. "Escaping."

When he sat in the open space next to Lizzy, across from Charlie, Charlie and Jane finally looked away from each other.

"Oh, hey." Charlie beamed at them. "Jane and I are planning our first date."

"Cool," said Will, pulling out his lunch. "Your sister's in a snit."

Charlie looked over at the Brat Pack table, frowned at Caroline, who was gesturing for him to come to the table, then shrugged. "She'll get over it."

"Doubtful." Will took a bite of sandwich.

For once, Lizzy figured she knew exactly how Caroline felt. "This is totally surreal."

When Will looked at her, smirked, she realized she'd said it out loud. "You'll get over it," he said.

When he turned back to his friend, a look passed between them that only confused Lizzy more.

"Did you...?" Charlie started to ask.

"Not yet," Will said quickly.

"Got it."

Whatever it was, she figured it wasn't her business anyway. And whatever was up with Will, she decided it must be a fluke, and tomorrow he'd go back to his usual table, even if it meant sitting with Caroline.

As she ate her own sandwich, another thought struck her that had her swallowing hard.

What if Jane went to sit at the Brat Pack table? Would that mean she'd be forced to sit alone, or worse, to sit with them, too?

Putting the cart before the horse, maybe. She'd deal with tomorrow tomorrow.

Some of the whispers around the courtyard wondering what was happening with Will and Charlie started reaching her ears, but the others didn't seem to notice. There were more than a few snickers about Caroline watching their table; curious, Lizzy glanced over at the Brat Pack.

The four at the table still looked a little confused, but all except for Caroline were still managing to power through their lunch. Caroline was seething, her glare obvious even across the courtyard.

If she didn't think it ridiculous, Lizzy would have thought Caroline was aiming that glare directly at her.

Seven

By the time Lizzy made it to AP Lit, news of the dance drama had morphed into talk of today's lunch drama. It was disconcerting to hear her name among the gossip, and associated with that of Will Darcy.

When she slid into her seat next to him, she turned and and gave him her most ferocious scowl.

He only raised his brows, smiled as though he already knew what her problem was and was amused by it.

"Can I help you with something?" he asked, all innocence.

"There's no way you don't already know the whole school is talking about the little stunt you pulled at lunch today."

"What of it?"

"I don't particularly care to be gossip fodder," she practically growled.

Unbothered, he tilted his head. "Neither do I. But it is what it is."

"That's it? That's all you have to say?"

He turned to face her more fully. "There isn't anything either of us can do about it, Elizabeth, except ignore it. It'll die down eventually."

It grated that he was right. For the most part, she didn't actually care about the gossip. What really concerned her was the idea someone besides Will might figure out she'd been at the dance as Cinderella. It was bad enough he'd figured it out, and though, despite herself, she felt she could trust him when he said he wouldn't tell, she thought it best not to bring that issue back to the forefront. Hopefully he was right, and everyone would move on to the next thing soon.

"My stepsisters are going to grill me when I get home," she grumbled. "Be forewarned, they will demand I get you to ask one of them out. They might even resort to blackmail, if they think they have any."

His brow rose. "Do they try to blackmail you often?"

Crap. Why had she told him that? A glance at him told her he was watching her, waiting for an answer, so she sighed, and braced herself.

"Every once in a while, they manage to break into my room and take something. It's why I've hidden my valuables, installed a deadbolt on my door, and always bring my laptop with me when I leave the house."

"That's messed up."

Both appreciating and resenting the mixture of horror and pity on his face, she shrugged. "Yes. But it is what it is," she said quietly, in echo of his words.

"Lizzy..."

He said it softly, almost warmly, like he meant to comfort her. Did he mean to comfort her? That didn't seem like something he'd do. She'd have to find out some other time, because before he could say anything else, their teacher rose from his desk and started class.

She did her best to pay attention, but the whole day had been a whirlwind of changes and emotional rollercoasters. Her mind felt like soup, reheated and going cold over and over again. Relief flooded her when she noticed there was only five minutes of class left, and she willed herself to listen to Mr. Goulding's closing remarks.

"So, for this next paper," he was saying, "You'll have three weeks to complete it, and you're going to be working with a partner."

A chorus of groans erupted from the students, including Lizzy. She hated group projects; she worked better alone, especially since working with groups meant she had to work around Frances.

Mr. Goulding held up his hands for peace. "I'll make it easy on you and assign your partners. You'll be working with the person next to you."

Lizzy's eyes widened. There were six rows, and she was in the second seat of row five. She whipped her head to look at the person in the second seat of row six.

"Hey, partner," Will said, even as Mr. Goulding used his arms to divide up the rows, making it clear who was working with who.

What even was this day?

At the end of the weirdest, most insane day of her high school career—after facing the expected interrogation from Kitty and Lydia and disappointing them with her lackluster answers—Lizzy sat on the window seat in her room, locked away for the night. She opened her phone to read Closet Poet's last message for the thousandth time.

Yes, they had agreed to see each other again, and she knew she was being a coward.

It was so easy, though. To ignore what she wasn't ready to face. To blame circumstances for her problems, even if she sometimes had more control than she thought she did.

It wasn't fair to him, she knew. Or to herself.

What would Cinderella do?

The question had her sitting up straighter, glancing at her bookshelf where her childhood book of fairytales sat on the bottom shelf. She remembered her dad's insistence Cinderella had courage, and faith; she trusted that everything would work out.

She started to type.

> Sorry I've been MIA.

She wanted to say more, but it would just be excuses, so she left it at that and after hovering her thumb for a moment, hit send.

His response came surprisingly quickly, and it shocked her more when he said:

CLOSET POET
It's okay. I understand.

> You do?

I think so. You're afraid. You're second guessing this.

> I guess I am. I'm afraid when you know who I am, you'll change your mind.

You don't need to worry about that.

The message came so immediately, and he sounded so sure. But how could he be so sure? She decided to ask him just that, and it was several minutes before his answer came this time.

She'd expected some kind of lengthy explanation, but instead he must have been debating whether or not to share information with her, because he simply said:

> Being with you at the dance was the happiest
> I've been in a while.

Her heart slammed against the walls of her chest as she read.

> Same for me.

> But you still doubt.

She did, but it had more to do with herself and her situation than it did him. Didn't it? Was she projecting her fears on him without realizing it?

She wasn't sure how long she contemplated this, anxiety making her limbs both lethargic and shaky at the same time, but when she looked at her phone again, she saw she had another message.

> I admit I have a similar fear. That you won't like
> what you find when you realize who I am.

But that was preposterous.

She nearly said so. But then she recalled Jane had asked her something similar. She had to accept it was possible she would be disappointed when she learned who Closet Poet was; thus, any reassurance on her part would be placating and hollow.

The only thing she could think to say was:

> I'm sorry if I made you fee that way.

> It's okay—for now. I will tell you who I am, but
> not until I feel we're both ready.

That's fair, I suppose. We can can decide when to tell each other who we are mutually.

There's something else.

Oh, boy. Did she even want to know?

…what?

I have your bracelet.

She was glad no one could see her, because she felt like her eyes were bugging out of her head. With euphorically relieved fingers, she managed to write:

Please explain.

I ran after you, and I saw it fall off before you left the gym. I detoured to pick it up.

OMG, thank you!

I'll give it back to you…when you're ready to find out who I am.

What? No way.

Excuse you? You can't hold it hostage.

If I give it to you now, you'll find out who I am. And if you learn who I am too soon, you might be disappointed. I don't want you to be disappointed.

For a moment she debated suggesting he find a way to give it to her without revealing himself, like trying to slip it in her locker or something. But even as she thought it, she dismissed it; the bracelet wouldn't fit through her locker slats, and she was not giving him her combination. Plus, he could easily find out whose locker it was.

Any other way risked it getting lost, so that was out.

She debated guilting him. Telling him the bracelet was her mother's, maybe even exaggerating and saying it was the only thing she had left of her. But as much as she wanted the bracelet back, even more, she could understand where he was coming from. After all, she was also afraid he'd be disappointed in her, Lizzy "Coffee Girl" Bennet.

But it was also lowering to realize he was afraid she would judge him too harshly. She'd thought she was a good judge of character, but maybe—just maybe—her years being used and steamrolled by Frances and the twins had made her jaded.

Not Cinderella approved, she thought with a wry smile.

> Alright, I'll bite. As long as you promise to keep it safe, you can hold onto it until we're ready.

Thank you.

It wasn't until later she considered he'd seen enough of her, and knew enough about her to potentially find out who she was if he wanted to. The idea made her impatient. But she'd just have to get used to it, she supposed, until Closet Poet was ready to reveal himself.

Or she did some digging of her own.

This time she heard him before she saw him—or maybe it was the hairs standing up on the back of her neck.

"I can't talk today, Colin," she said, deliberately leaving her locker open as a barrier.

"You've had time to consider my application," he said. "I expect a more positive response from you when I ask again."

"Then you need to adjust your expectations. I already gave you my answer."

"Yes, but I realized you must not have been serious. Many girls like to say no when they secretly mean to say yes. I concluded you just want to keep me in suspense by teasing me, which I know is a delightful habit of yours."

Unsure whether to be annoyed or insulted, Lizzy slowly closed her locker, then, since insult was winning out, spoke as carefully and steadily as possible. "That doesn't mean I don't know when to be serious, Colin. You deserved a straightforward answer, so I gave you one. The answer is still no."

"But I—"

"I'd listen to her if I were you."

Lizzy stilled, turned her head over her shoulder to look at Will, who was sending a disturbingly black look in Colin's direction, his dark hair perfectly wind-tousled. She'd always thought he made a picture, but there was something about the piercing glare on his face aimed at Colin that had her stomach melting into goo with an internal sigh.

Wait, what? What was she thinking?

While Colin spluttered, Will turned his gaze to her, and his face softened considerably. "Good morning, Lizzy."

"Will."

"Do you have time to meet up later today?"

He ignored Colin, but Colin was not easily ignored.

"Unbelievable!" Colin gasped. "I'd heard rumors you and your, admittedly very pretty, friend were reaching above their social sphere, but this is beyond the pale."

"'Reaching above their social sphere?'" Will blinked, his face darkening again. "What is this, an Austen novel? It's the twenty-first century. Lizzy can talk to whomever she damn well pleases."

"But why would you lower yourself to be with Elizabeth when surely you wish to unite yourself with Caroline?"

The question was so earnest, so genuinely concerned, it was almost amusing—almost. Lizzy could have sworn she saw fire erupt in Will's eyes as he took a couple rather menacing steps toward Colin, who instinctively shrunk back.

"You don't get to tell me what I want," he growled.

Since he looked like he was about to pummel Colin's face in, Lizzy stepped up to Will's side, pressed a hand to his chest. Ignoring the feel of solid muscle through his t-shirt, and his rapidly beating heart under her palm, she directed a deceptively calm look at Colin.

"We're partners for a paper in AP Lit," she told him. "He was asking me when I'd be available to work on it."

She pushed lightly at Will's chest, and he got the hint. Though he still glowered at Colin, he stepped back, allowing her to drop her hand.

Though she was surprised by how much she missed the contact, she shook it off and deliberately directed his attention to her. "I work until five-thirty," she told him.

"And I have practice until five-thirty, so that works out. Where do you want to meet?"

She glanced at her peripheral, and saw that, thankfully, Colin had left. "I usually go to the public library after work, unless Jane and I have plans."

He nodded. "Sounds good."

"Will?" She stopped him before he could walk off. "You could have just asked me about this in class, you know."

He seemed to hear the unspoken question, and smiled a little.

"I was going to ask you about it at lunch, but I heard what that guy was saying."

"So you thought you'd be my white knight?"

"I thought I'd be your friend."

For a moment she could only stare at him; when he didn't say anything else, she supposed she had to believe him.

"Well, thanks, but I think you made it worse. Now he's got something else to rag on me about."

"Want me to have a talk with him?"

"Absolutely not." She shook her head with finality. "I do not need him thinking you're interested in me and blabbing about it to the whole school. I'll handle him."

Like you've handled him so far? Will thought, resolving to ignore that directive. It looked like this Colin guy didn't know how to take no; either he had no real respect for Elizabeth—or more likely, the female population in general—or he was just plain obtuse. Either way, he needed a bit of a boot in the ass, and it would be his pleasure to dole it out.

Eight

THOUGH HE'D IMPLIED it that morning, Lizzy was still surprised when Will and Charlie sat with her and Jane at their usual table at lunch.

On the one hand, she was incredibly happy for Jane; she and Charlie hardly noticed others around them as they talked, and Jane had already told her they'd be going to the movies later for their first date.

Jane had even shared her portion of their lunchtime snack—sweet chili Doritos today—with Charlie.

On the other, it was frustrating, because she wanted to talk about Closet Poet with Jane, but even if Jane wasn't absorbed in Charlie, they'd have no privacy to talk about it in front of Charlie and Will. Will, of course, was a source of frustration himself.

Oh, he'd been playing nice, and she couldn't deny he was pleasant to be around when he exerted himself.

But she was seeing more of him than she ever expected to. It was like a switch was flipped, throwing her and Jane into the world of the Brat Pack, and she couldn't help feeling like someone would turn the switch off soon.

Or the wiring would short-circuit.

Maybe Charlie would stick around, but Will probably wanted to get back to his usual routine of ignoring them and brooding into his black coffee. Already he was looking pretty bored, scrolling through his phone as he chewed his panini.

Admittedly, she was bored, too, without Jane to talk to. Crunching into a Dorito as she eyed Will, who sat across from her, she wondered if she could have a little fun with him by making him talk. As she considered, he looked up from his phone, lifted a brow.

"What?"

Darn—she'd been caught staring again. Covering her embarrassment by folding her arms on the table and leaning forward, she said, "I've been wondering something."

"What's that?"

"You were at the dance. Why didn't you accept the crown?"

He set down his phone, shrugged. "Didn't want it."

She tilted her head. "Why wouldn't you want to be homecoming king?"

"Would you want to be homecoming queen?" He mirrored her position, green eyes boring into her in a way that once again made her feel like he understood more about her than he'd let on.

"Well, no," she faltered, and she knew what he would ask next.

"Why not?"

"You mean, aside from it being an overinflated popularity contest?" she quipped, then sighed when he only inclined his head, waited patiently for her answer. "I guess I just wouldn't want the attention."

One corner of his lips curved as he nodded. "There you go."

When she thought about it, she supposed it made sense. Sure, he was popular, but it was mostly by virtue of who he was, and how hot he was. He himself had never made any effort to impress anybody—in fact, he actively discouraged positive interactions. And though she'd noted his brooding scowl many a time, she'd never considered that maybe it was the attention he was displeased by.

"To what does this question tend?" He asked her when she didn't reply.

"I guess I'm just trying to understand you a little better."

Now he smiled more fully. "And why is that?"

She met his eyes. "Because you're a puzzle. And I haven't met a puzzle I didn't want to solve."

"Well, let me know when you've got me figured out."

"Oh, no, that's not the goal."

"It isn't?"

"No. I have no interest in giving myself impossible tasks."

He chuckled. "Am I that hard to read?"

Smiling, she shook her head. "Sometimes. But I meant...do you have yourself figured out?"

"Uh..." His brow furrowed. "No, I guess I don't."

"Exactly. So how can I figure out what even you don't know?"

"That's a good question."

She smirked. "That's why I asked it."

"Okay, smart ass." He smirked back, and nipped a Dorito from her bag.

And that was how the king of brooding, Will Darcy, made the intrepid Elizabeth Bennet laugh. Neither of them noticed the furious gaze of Caroline Bingley as she watched them from her table across the courtyard.

Will noticed his heartbeat kicked up a notch when he saw Lizzy sitting on a bench outside the library, doing something on her phone as she waited for him. It would be his first time truly alone with her—as himself, anyway—and he had to admit he was nervous. He was still figuring out how to play this—how to be more himself without making it outright obvious he was Closet Poet.

He'd nearly told her last night, even typed out the words. But something held him back, made him delete the words.

It wouldn't be fair to hold his identity back from her if she knew he knew she was Lit Fairy. And again, it might be obvious he was Closet Poet if she caught on why he was suddenly interested in spending time with her.

And he wasn't sure how she would handle that. He'd meant it when he said he didn't want her to be disappointed. In a way, this paper was a blessing since it gave him a good excuse to be around her, talk to her.

He'd just have to make sure she liked him enough to forgive him when he told her. That she'd understand.

"Hey," he said when he approached her.

"Hey." She tucked her phone away, rose to go inside.

Since she clearly had a routine, he just followed her to a quiet table at the end of one of the stacks on the second floor, sat down across from her.

"So," she said, pulling out her laptop and notebook. "Obviously, we need to choose a topic before we can do anything else. Thoughts?"

"A few." He tapped a pen against his own notebook. Their assignment was to analyze a theme from either the novel or one of the two short stories they'd read so far that semester, and a few of the suggested prompts on the list Mr. Goulding had given them stood out. "What are you leaning toward?"

"I'm torn between early feminist themes and hysteria in 'The

Yellow Wallpaper' or comparing elements of the myth of Prometheus and their use in *Frankenstein*."

He pursed his lips. "I may have already done a paper on 'The Yellow Wallpaper' in AP English last year. So while I'm sure we could do that one justice, I think it'd be more fun to do the Prometheus one."

When she gave him a slow smile, he raised a brow. "What?"

She shrugged. "I just love that you're as much of a nerd as I am. Modern Prometheus it is."

They got to work thinking of examples in the text that compared to the version of the Prometheus myth in which Prometheus is responsible for human creation, and, as they wrapped up, decided they could research outside sources next time.

As they headed out, parted ways, he noticed she was walking down the sidewalk instead of to the parking lot. When he called out to her, she hesitated before turning around.

"What?"

"Where are you going?"

"Home," she said like was obvious.

His brow furrowed. "On foot?"

"Yep. I walked here."

"Okay, well, it wouldn't be very gentlemanly of me to let you walk home alone." He held up his keys. "Can I give you a lift?"

"No, that's o—"

"Lizzy. Let me give you a ride."

He used the tone he sometimes took with his sister, the one that said he would brook no opposition because he was doing what was best, for her protection and his peace of mind. Whether she caught on to the subtext he couldn't say, but she seemed to to understand he wasn't just insisting.

"Alright," she acquiesced, and silently followed him to his car.

He watched her as she hopped into the passenger's seat of his sleek black truck, observed the way she settled carefully, like she was afraid to touch anything. He asked her address, plugged it into his GPS.

It was quiet as they pulled away from the library. He wanted to tell her she wouldn't break anything, but she spoke before he could.

"Well, that was surprisingly productive," she commented.

"Why surprisingly?"

"Well…" Her lips thinned as she looked away. "I guess I expected to have to do most of the work. That's what usually happens in group projects."

"Same, actually."

"Really?"

"Really." He started the car. "I make no secret of the fact I'm a straight A student; most people just don't think to ask about my grades."

She nodded slowly. "Like how Caroline didn't know you take AP classes."

He gave her a reassuring smile. "Like I said, it's not a secret, but I never bother to correct anyone either."

"Well, I guess why would you?" she wondered. "Your grades aren't really anyone's business."

"True." As he drove, he thought of something most people didn't know about her. "Can I ask you something?"

Her brow quirked. "I suppose."

"Why aren't you on the softball team?"

Though his eyes were on the road, he could see her head whip around out of the corner of his eye.

"What? What do you mean?"

"So, last week, Charlie and I were near the softball field when someone hit a ball over the fence. He recognized the pitcher as Jane and assumed the batter was you. Was it?"

"...Yes. You're the one who threw the ball back?"

"Yeah. Charlie said Jane is on the softball team. But you're not?"

She gave a long suffering sigh. "I'm afraid that would be impossible."

"Why?" he pressed. "Something tells me you've got the skills."

Her jaw set, she sighed again. "Frances would never allow it."

The only place he could recall hearing the name was the name of the café—and then it clicked. "Is that your stepmom?"

"Yep." She popped the *P* for emphasis. "Frances deems softball too dirty a sport for a girl, and besides which, I wouldn't have time anyway since my job is more important."

At a stoplight, he turned to take in her face, tried to determine whether or not she was serious. "She really believes that?"

"Sure. But I personally think she also enjoys depriving me of things that might bring me joy."

He thought over what she'd said about her stepsisters the other day, and about what Lit Fairy had revealed about her father's death and her home life.

"Why don't you leave?" he asked. "There's got to be something you can do."

"It's a long story." She sounded defeated, until she frowned at him. "Why do you care anyway?"

Well, he couldn't very well tell her the main reason he cared. But he could still be truthful.

"What, I'm not allowed to care what happens to you?" He asked, letting some of his annoyance show. "We may not exactly be friends, Elizabeth, but that doesn't mean we couldn't be. And only someone completely devoid of compassion wouldn't feel for you."

"I don't want your pity."

"Well, too bad," he shot back. "I'm allowed be sorry about the situation you're in, just as you're allowed be sorry you're in it. Deal."

She huffed, folded her arms as she looked away. He decided to take that as a reluctant agreement—or she was agreeing to disagree. He supposed he'd have to take it for now.

When he pulled up to the curb outside her house, she'd already unbuckled her seatbelt and reached for the door. Wrenching it open, she didn't look back at him as she stepped out.

It was a nice house, he noted, and bigger than he'd expected. A two-story Tudor, fairytale-esque with its lush rosebushes under the front windows. But it definitely leaned toward the Grimm fairytale side with all the gnomes lining the walkway, and odd stone statues littered throughout the yard, like Medusa had been hired to decorate. It was a bit jarring, especially when compared with the bright pink door.

Both the yard decor and the door, he suspected, were Frances's touch.

"Bye, Elizabeth," he said, adding a little teasing to his tone.

She paused with her hand on the door, gave him a steely glare. But she said, "Thanks for the ride," before slamming the door shut, and walking up the driveway.

He chuckled to himself, watching until she made it inside before pulling back out onto the street.

She wasn't used to people pitying her, and the fact he did obviously disconcerted her. He wasn't sure where that put him, but it was an interesting progression in their relationship. He thought he'd managed to get across he wasn't some cold, selfish rich guy, at least. He could only hope her impression of him was improving.

Nine

HAD HE MISCALCULATED? Will wondered for the hundredth time. He hadn't seen Elizabeth yet that day, so he had no idea if she was still annoyed with him or not. Though, if she was, she could be avoiding him. And if that was the case, how could he fix it?

As he stood at his locker before lunch, he considered finding that Colin guy and having a little talk with him. He'd already second-guessed that idea a few times, and not just because he didn't know where to find the guy, except perhaps at Lizzy's locker.

Lizzy had asked him not to interfere, and she might get annoyed if he did it anyway. So, though it went against the grain, he decided he'd hold off for now. He could always act if things escalated.

Plus, she couldn't avoid him forever. They had a paper to work on. And he'd have to make sure they talked about when to meet up over lunch, or before or after class again; there was no way they could exchange numbers without her realizing she already had his number, and why.

As he pulled out a book, someone leaned into the locker next to him, and he turned his head to see a pretty brunette with her body slunk against the locker, one arm above her head, in a manner she must have thought was coy. She wore a ruffled tank top and a miniskirt that had the potential to break the dress code. He recognized her as one of the Gardiner twins that was always trying to cozy up to Caroline like they were friends.

"Hi, Will," she said breathily, winking.

"Uh. Hi, Lydia." He put the book in his backpack. She wasn't the first girl to try hitting on him, and he doubted she'd be the last. She got an A for effort, though.

Slinging his backpack over his shoulder, he reached for the locker door. In a surprisingly fast move, Lydia shot out an arm, simultaneously closing the locker and turning her body so she was facing him, back pressed against the lockers in a way that puffed out her chest a little.

She batted her eyelashes. He stepped back.

"Now that you and Caroline are old news, I thought you might want to have a little fun with someone...more fun," she purred, a silky smile curving red-painted lips. He saw some lipstick stained one of her teeth, wondered if she'd noticed.

"I'm good, thanks."

Her smile turned to a pout, but before she said anything else, a voice called out, "Lydia!"

Another girl, slightly taller, and with dark blonde hair rushed over and looked between him and Lydia with widened eyes.

Great, he thought. Double trouble.

"What are you doing? We agreed I'd ask him out first." Then she seemed to remember he was standing right there, and turned an overly bright smile on him; at least she was dressed more appropriately, in skinny jeans and a blouse, and her makeup less garish. "Hi, Will."

He blinked, but she only continued to smile at him. Meanwhile, Lydia rolled her eyes.

"No, you suggested it, but I didn't agree. Why would he waste his time with you when he could have *moi?*"

Kitty sniffed. "Because I'm the older, more mature one."

Lydia snorted, finally pushing off the lockers and standing normally. "Fourteen minutes might make you older, but I'm the prettier one."

Will did not foresee this situation playing out well. Kitty was glaring at Lydia, while Lydia looked smug, and since the Gardiner twins were known for their catfights, he considered just turning and walking away.

"Why don't we let Will decide?" Kitty posed, and turned to him expectantly. Lydia likewise turned to face him, batted her eyelashes again.

"Well, which of us do you want to go out with?"

The word 'neither' was on the tip of his tongue when a third voice, thankfully one he recognized, cut in.

"I'm pretty sure he has better things to do than go out with either of you," Lizzy said as she stepped up beside him. He couldn't help noticing how cute she looked today, in a simple black sundress dotted with tiny daisies, and a long golden yellow cardigan. The look wasn't complete, of course, without her signature Converse.

Lydia sneered. "What do you know, *Lose*-y?"

Lizzy smirked as that telltale brow arched. "Punny."

"What are you even doing here?" Kitty asked, though with a less antagonistic tone.

"I was just passing by, but I figured I'd return a favor and rescue Will from your clutches."

Will's lips twitched, but thankfully neither twin was paying attention. Kitty scrunched up her face, but Lydia, as per usual, wasn't one to back down.

"He doesn't need rescuing. He was about to tell us he wants *me* to be his girlfriend."

Well that escalated quickly—leaping from trying to ask him on a date to insisting on being his girlfriend. What was it with these two?

He realized all three pairs of eyes had turned to him, but only Lizzy's were devoid of expectation. Apparently she wasn't going to prevent him from answering.

"Uh, sorry ladies," he started, trying to think of a way to be diplomatic about it. "There's a guy somewhere out there for each of you, but I'm not him."

Kitty's bright smile turned down into disappointment, but she seemed to accept his answer. Lydia, on the other hand, once again proved her obstinacy. She scowled and turned a mutinous glare on Elizabeth.

"You always ruin everything!" she shouted. Anyone who hadn't been watching the confrontation before certainly was now.

Lizzy only gave Lydia a bland stare. "Pretty sure I had nothing to do with it. Will's a big boy—he can make his own decisions."

He was about to agree, but Lydia plowed on.

"You think you're so clever, so much better than us?" Chin high, nose in the air, she cocked a hip. "Well, you're not. You're nobody. Just a sad orphan girl no guy would ever want."

Eyes deadpan with Lydia's, Lizzy barely batted an eye. "Well," she said, her tone almost bored. "Glad we've established that."

Lizzy might be able to brush it off, but there was no way he could let the insult stand.

"Lydia." She must have missed the sternness in his voice, because she immediately replaced her glare with a smile as she turned back to him. "There's no reason to take your disappointment out on Elizabeth. My answer would have been the same even if she wasn't here."

He looked her up and down, letting some of the disgust he felt for her show. "I could never be with someone so petty and mean —which is one of the reasons I've never been interested in Caroline."

Kitty squeaked, her eyes, if possible, getting even wider. Lydia's jaw dropped, and she finally turned her narrowed gaze on him instead of Elizabeth, whom he turned to, waving his arm out to the side with a flourish.

"Shall we?"

Thankfully, she wasn't annoyed by his defense of her, and offered him a small smile. "I believe we shall."

She took a step, then stopped as she turned her head to look back at Lydia, flick her eyes over her face. Lydia sneered; Lizzy smirked.

"You have lipstick in your teeth."

Lydia's eyes went wide with horror, and her screech followed him and Elizabeth down the hall as they headed toward the courtyard.

Eyes were still on them, he noticed as they entered. Maybe because it was the first time they'd arrived to lunch together.

"Should I apologize?" he asked as they sat. Charlie and Jane weren't there yet, so he thought he'd take the opportunity to apologize while they were still alone. "That scene, and the fact that we just walked to lunch together, are bound to start another round of rumors."

Her brows drew together a little as she tilted her head. "None of that was your fault. Besides, if anyone should apologize it's me, since my stepsisters were harassing you."

"What?" He blinked. "The Gardiner twins are your stepsisters?"

She paused in the act of taking a sandwich out of her lunch bag. "You didn't know?"

"No. I..." he considered a moment. "I guess I thought they'd have the same last name as you."

She shrugged. "They might have, if my dad had lived longer. But he died only a couple months after he married Frances, so no paperwork was ever filed. Though I have to say, I'm glad we don't share a name."

He nodded absently, his mind automatically fitting more puzzle pieces together. When he looked back at her, she was frowning at him. He was about to ask what that look was for, but then he recalled their last conversation.

"Don't worry, I'm not pitying you," he assured her. "I was just thinking that it all makes so much more sense now."

"What does?"

"You. Having to put up with them."

"Ah."

Her lips quirked and she might have said more, but they were interrupted by the arrival, not of their expected friends, but an unexpected one of his.

"Hey." Ricky swung a leg over the bench, slumped into the seat next to Will as he plopped his backpack on the ground. "Mind if I join you?"

Will took a page out of Lizzy's book and lifted a brow, flicked a glance toward the fountain table. "That bad, huh?"

"Dude, you have no idea. Caroline is like, on a rampage or something. Even Anne and Lou are starting to think she's lost it." Shaking his head, Ricky pulled a brown paper bag from his backpack, dropped it on the table. "I thought maybe I could steer her attention to me, you know? But she's stuck on you, bro."

Cheerful as ever, he slapped Will's chest with the back of his hand.

Chuckling, Will just shrugged. "No, she's stuck on the idea of me."

"What I'm curious about," Elizabeth cut in, "Is this 'rampage' you speak of."

Ricky blinked, as though he'd just remembered she was there, then grinned at her. "Hey! If it isn't the lovely Lizzy."

Her brows shot up her forehead. "Oh, so I'm 'lovely Lizzy' now? Not Coffee Girl?"

Ricky at least had the decency to look abashed, the tips of his ears pinking a little as he shrugged. "Yeah, um, sorry about that."

Then he looked around, checking to make sure no one was listening before he leaned forward and said in a near whisper, "For real though, that was the best pumpkin spice latte I've ever had."

When a corner of Lizzy's mouth turned up and her eyes sparkled with humor, Will knew she was softening toward his friend. "Well, thank you."

"Sorry we're late. Hey, Ricky." Charlie stepped up to the table, and sat on the other side of Will; Jane, close behind him, sat across from him, next to Lizzy.

"'Sup, dude?" Ricky muffled through a mouthful of sandwich, then swallowed before saying, "Your sister's off her rocker."

Charlie merely shrugged. "So what else is new?"

"Maybe she's still heartbroken," Jane suggested, handing Lizzy a packet of Cheez-Its.

"Trust me." Charlie laid a hand over hers. "She was never heartbroken. She's just pissy she isn't getting what she wants."

"It's about time," Will muttered.

"You might want to watch out," said Elizabeth, popping a Cheez-It in her mouth. "Angry people aren't always wise, and someone as petty as her isn't going to let your defection go so easily. She may just be biding her time."

Jane blinked at her. "You make it sound like a war."

"Nah. It's just high school."

CLOSET POET

Are you avoiding me?

The text sat alone in Lizzy's messages, staring at her accusingly. Blowing out a breath, she picked up her phone, considered how to respond.

Was she avoiding him? Probably. She didn't think she was doing it on purpose, though. She'd been a little distracted the last couple days, namely by an objectively handsome, surprisingly companionable guy with killer green eyes, whose name rhymed with Dill Warcy.

Ugh. She must be tired—she only thought loopy thoughts when she needed sleep.

Regardless, she recognized that honesty was usually the best policy.

> I don't really know what to say to you.

I suppose that's fair.

> Where do we go from here, Poet? Logically, it would make sense to try to meet in person again at some point. But it seems like we're both too afraid to do that right now.

Agreed. I guess we'll just have to decide it's worth it, and risk it.

> When?

She thought maybe he'd have to think about it for a bit, but his response came after only a few seconds.

Soon, Fairy. Soon.

Ten

THURSDAY MORNING FLEW by in a daze. Life was getting a little more complicated than she was used to, Lizzy grumbled to herself. Not only did she have to deal with school, work, and her stepfamily as usual, but she also had to deal with the confusion surrounding her feelings for Closet Poet and her newfound friendship—if she could call it that—with Will Darcy.

Normally, she was able to keep a cool head, but she couldn't deny she was starting to get a little stressed.

At least she'd have somewhat of a break over the weekend. She was busy with work, and Will was busy with football, so they'd agreed to research some sources, then pool their notes the next time they met up, which wouldn't be until Monday.

They worked well together, she thought with some surprise as she sat at their table at lunch. She'd known, on some level, that he was intelligent—he'd often been in her AP classes over the years. And that was, after all, where their sort of rivalry had begun, battling it out in class discussions marked with debate and wit. Those debates had never gotten heated, but they'd pushed each other; she'd thought they were pushing each other's buttons, but maybe they'd actually helped each other to thrive.

Academically, anyway.

"Hi."

She blinked herself out of her musings, looked up to see Anne standing before her, books clutched to her chest.

Lizzy didn't bother to hide her confusion. "Hi?"

"Um." Anne tucked a strand of her coppery hair behind her ear. "Would it be alright if I sat with you guys?"

Lizzy glanced at the fountain table, but it was empty. When she looked back at Anne, took in her fidgeting stance and the apprehensive look on her face, she took pity on her and shrugged.

"I doubt anyone would mind."

Though she smiled in relief, Lizzy could tell by the way she held herself that Anne was still tense. She sat across from Lizzy with her shoulders a little hunched, and her knee bounced repetitively under the table.

As a peace offering, Lizzy offered her some of the Fritos she'd brought for herself and Jane; Anne accepted a handful with a tentative smile.

The others seemed to arrive all at once. Charlie and Jane smiled at Anne as they sat by Lizzy, Will raised a brow but nodded at her, and Ricky, who sat next to her, beamed.

"Well, hey Annie. You breaking ranks, too?"

Anne turned her big gray eyes to him with a surprisingly playful smile. "I guess I am."

Ah, Lizzy thought. So that was her motivation. But she was proven wrong when she learned a few minutes later that Ricky and Anne were cousins. And if she wasn't mistaken, Ricky was actually a little protective of Anne, something Lizzy understood when Anne had to be prodded to speak.

They talked of inconsequential things, and Lizzy was pleasantly surprised by the camaraderie among their group. Though a part of her missed just getting to spend time with Jane, and though she couldn't say they were all friends, it wasn't nearly as much of a trial as she'd thought it'd be.

With the revelation that Will wasn't as aloof as he pretended to be, she had to be open to the idea that neither were Ricky or Anne what they appeared. Ricky was actually quite easy to talk to, probably because he was so easygoing, while Anne was much quieter than she'd expected.

Now that she'd set her judgments of them aside, it occurred to Lizzy Caroline's personality was pretty dominant. That maybe her nature overshadowed those of her friends'.

This theory was only reinforced as Anne came out of her shell over the course of the next couple days. Once she understood the others weren't going to force their opinions on her, or try to talk over her, she was a bit more vocal, though still hesitant.

Toward the end of the lunch period on Friday, she'd ventured to speak half a dozen times.

"Oh, Lizzy." Jane turned to her with worried eyes. "I forgot to tell you I made plans with Charlie for after school today, before the game."

"Oh. That's okay, I can walk to the café."

"What are you talking about?" Will asked.

"Lizzy doesn't have a car," Jane explained before Lizzy could assure him it was nothing. "She catches a ride with me to school, and I usually drive her to work after."

When Will met Lizzy's gaze, she knew he was thinking about how she'd tried to walk home from the library; she also knew what he would offer even before he said, "Well, I could drive you."

"It's fine," she assured him. "I can walk. It's nothing I haven't done before."

"How long does it take you?"

She frowned, already understanding where he was going with that argument. "About a half hour, but—"

"It'll only take me ten minutes to drive you. It'd be silly to walk."

"I like walking," she insisted.

He gave her a knowing smile. "Stop being so stubborn. It's not a big deal."

She pouted, noticing the amused glances of the others at the table, and huffed. "Fine."

Satisfied, he smiled. "Fine," he echoed, and popped a potato chip in his mouth.

When had he stolen that?

Will could tell Lizzy was wary when he found her at her locker at the end of the day. She was doing a good job of hiding she was nervous about him driving her to work, but he could tell by the way her fingers tapped her locker door as she pulled out a book that something was bugging her.

"Ready?" he asked when he reached her.

She nearly dropped the book as she was shoving it in her bag. "What?"

She hadn't heard him come up, and he'd totally thrown her off. Maybe it was sadistic of him to enjoy discomposing her, but he couldn't help the smirk that curved at his lips. "For me to drive you to work."

"Yes. Why don't I just meet you in the parking lot?" she muttered, annoyance coloring her tone.

"You don't know where I parked."

She blinked. "That's why I said at the parking lot, and not at your car."

She shut her locker, started down the hall. He was at her side with only a couple strides.

"It's almost like you don't want to be seen with me," he teased.

She sighed, but it seemed like it was more out of resignation than annoyance.

"Fine. But don't blame me if another round of rumors about us starts circulating."

Make that *when*, he thought as he led her to his car. Even without looking, he could feel multiple pairs of eyes on them—but he'd only play into it if he looked, so he didn't, and as if by the same instinct, neither did she. He watched her as they climbed in, so he saw it wasn't until she'd tossed her bag on the floor and buckled herself into the passenger's seat that she took a peek out of her peripheral.

He did the same as he put the key in the ignition. As he'd suspected, there were plenty of people staring at the truck, most of them gaping or pointing in shock. But some of them were glaring.

Namely, Caroline and Louisa.

Lizzy must have noticed, too, because she was frowning in that direction, so he said, "Don't mind Caroline. She'll probably throw a tantrum at some point, but as I recall, you were rather entertained by her last one."

He trusted she'd understand the reference to the scene Caroline made in the café before the dance.

"That is my fondest memory of her." Lizzy's lips twitched as he started the car. "However, it doesn't mean I'm looking forward to one possibly being directed at me. I'd rather remain a spectator."

"You and me both."

They drove to the café in silence, which he figured was pure stubbornness on her part. When they were only a few minutes away, he said, "It doesn't bother me, you know."

"What doesn't?"

"That people talk about us. As a couple."

"Well, goody for you."

For a moment he thought she was going to leave it at that, but then she shifted in her seat, turned brightened eyes on him. "It's easier for you because you're Mr. Popular, and you're a guy. You can slum it with whoever you want, and no one will think less of you for it. They might even congratulate you on the conquest. But me? I'm throwing myself at you, a shameless slut, reaching above my station—you name it. You might be a duck, but I've spent all of high school avoiding the pond; now because of you, I'm all wet."

He let out a short laugh, grinned at her. "Is that so?"

He knew she understood how that had sounded when a delightful pink flush colored her cheeks. "You know what I mean, jerkwad."

"I do." He chuckled again. "Did you just call me a duck?"

"It was a metaphor!" She turned away and folded her arms across her chest, refusing to look at him as she explained. "Gossip rolls off you like water off a duck."

"You could be a duck, too, you know." His lips quirked as he said it, and she must have heard the amusement in his voice, because she huffed.

"I can't believe we're having this conversation."

He laughed quietly once more before straightening his features, turning the conversation serious again. "I do get it, though."

And he did. Gossip could be cruel for anyone, but for someone who wasn't used to it, it could be hard to swallow. But if there was one thing he knew about Lizzy Bennet, it was that she was strong.

"I know it's harder for you. And I know I could say nothing anyone says matters, and it still wouldn't mitigate feeling ridiculed. But they won't ridicule you."

"Oh, yeah?"

"Yeah. Because the Elizabeth Bennet I know is a force to be reckoned with. I have no doubts you can handle whatever comes your way."

Out of the corner of his eye, he could see her arms loosen, her hands fall into her lap. "Oh, yeah?" she said, quietly this time.

"It might seem daunting now. But something tells me most of what anyone says would amuse you more than upset you. You're more of a duck than you think."

A quiet snort escaped her, but she didn't say anything else.

"And if you really need it," he continued. "A plus to being Mr. Popular is when I tell people to back off, they usually do. If I make it clear no one messes with you, they won't."

"Why would you do that?" Her voice sounded a little strangled, and he wondered if she was holding back tears, or if she was just annoyed with him again.

Maybe it was too much too soon, but...screw it. He didn't want her to doubt his friendship.

"I thought we established I'm allowed to care about you, Lizzy."

He heard her intake of breath, and the smug part of him hoped she was rethinking her statement about his lack of charm, at least when it came to her. She still said nothing, but this time he let it go. They were only a couple blocks from the café, and he'd rather have his last statement on her mind.

As he pulled up to the curb, she didn't rush like last time, just methodically unbuckled her seatbelt and picked up her bag.

"Thanks for the ride." She almost grumbled it, like she was really saying she'd rather have walked barefoot over Legos than been coerced into letting him drive her around.

He held back a smirk. "See you on Monday, Elizabeth."

"See you." She opened the door, hopped out. When she'd

slung her bag on her shoulder, laid a hand on the car door, she paused to look back at him. "Good luck. At the game tonight."

He smiled. "Thanks."

Duty fulfilled, she nodded, and went inside. Still smiling, he drove off.

Let her ponder that all weekend.

Eleven

WHEN WILL WANDERED into the kitchen the next morning, his father was already up, sitting at the kitchen table with a mug of black coffee and the newspaper.

"Good morning, Will," he said, his voice deceptively calm.

Will merely flicked a glance at his father's steady gaze on his way to the counter. "Morning," he grumbled, going straight for the coffee pot.

"You played a good game last night," his dad said as he got down a mug, filled it to the brim.

Good game was an understatement—it'd been neck and neck in the first half, but they'd won fourteen to seven, a victory that meant they'd be playing in the championship game on Friday. But of course, good was was never good enough for Robert Darcy.

Since he could hear the 'but' in the statement, Will turned, leaned his back against the counter. Eyeing his dad over the rim of the mug as he inhaled that first fog-clearing sip, he simply said, "Thanks."

Robert laid aside his paper. "You seemed a little distracted, though."

And there it was.

Maybe he had been distracted. He'd been thinking about Elizabeth, after all. But he felt like he was making progress with her, which had made him happy—and that happiness was likely what had made him play well, despite his mind not being totally on the game.

He shrugged. "I was in a good mood."

Robert's brows rose a little as he continued to watch his son. "That may be, but perhaps you should focus less on whatever—or whoever—put you in such a good mood, and more on the game at hand."

"If I wasn't in such a good mood, I wouldn't have played as well," Will countered. He wouldn't dignify the advice by mentioning Elizabeth, or her affect on him. "Are you suggesting I should be in a bad mood on Friday?"

"No, of course not." Robert narrowed his eyes in a way that suggested Will was being ridiculous. "But I'm sure Caroline would understand where your focus needs to be this week."

Will sputtered out a laugh. His dad seriously thought he was happy because of Caroline? Well, maybe that could work in his favor. If he played it right, maybe he'd think Caroline was inadvertently the reason for his good mood.

"What's so funny?" Robert's frown was a mixture of confusion and annoyance.

"That you think I have any interest in Caroline." Will smiled, took another sip of coffee. "In fact, I told her straight out I'm not interested in her."

"Oh." His dad blinked, then smiled a little. "Well, good."

"Good?"

"Yes. That girl is..."

When Robert trailed off, but clearly could not think of something diplomatic to say, Will just smirked and nodded.

"Yes. She is."

"Well." His mission clearly accomplished, Robert rose, tucked his paper under his arm, and picked up his coffee. "Now that that's settled, I expect there to be no hindrances to your focus. Friday's game is of the utmost importance. I've got the head coach from Stanford coming to see you, and if you impress him your spot is guaranteed."

Will fought to keep a straight face, aided by pressing his mug to his lips, taking a long gulp. Since his father seemed to be expecting an answer, he swallowed and said, "Understood."

When his dad nodded, left the room, Will sagged against the counter.

Needless to say, his good mood was gone.

Normally, after a conversation with his dad like this one, he'd message Lit Fairy, maybe take a walk. And he could do that, he supposed.

But he had a better idea.

With the morning coffee rush over, midmorning on a Saturday was relatively slow at the café. Lizzy expected things would pick up again closer to the brunch hour, but for now, she took the opportunity to enjoy the quiet.

While she worked, she thought about Closet Poet's radio silence. He hadn't messaged her in two days, which was the longest they'd gone without talking in several months. To be fair, though, she hadn't reached out to him either. Guilt and confusion pricked at her heart, like little needles in a pincushion.

She still didn't know what to say to him. And to top it off, she realized she actually hadn't thought of him much over the past couple days. Sure, there was a lot going on at school, but deep down she suspected there was another reason her thoughts had drifted elsewhere.

An absolutely ridiculous reason she'd prefer not to dwell on.

In the middle of her ruminating, the bell over the door chimed, and she was surprised to see Will meander through the door. He was frowning, as per usual, but there was something different about this frown.

Wait, why would she think that? She didn't know him well enough to tell the difference between one frown or another.

Did she?

As it was a little too close to that sneaking suspicion she had, she shook the thought away. Regardless, he seemed irritated, and perhaps a little lost. When he walked up to the counter, she put on her customer service smile. "What can I get you?"

He was silent for a moment, staring at the menu board as though he hadn't heard her, or possibly was ignoring her. She was about to ask again when he looked right at her.

"You know what irks me?" he asked, apropos of nothing.

A number of snarky comments ran through her head, but something about his genuine distress tugged at her. She wracked her brain for a proper reply, but couldn't guess what had put him in a mood. "People asking you what you want?"

"No. People *telling* me what I want."

She was sure her face revealed her skepticism and confusion. "Why would *you* let someone else tell you how to live your life?"

He scoffed, a humorless sound of frustration she was familiar with herself. "You've never met my dad."

"Ah." She nodded. "No, but I definitely know what it's like to have an overbearing guardian. To feel you have no say in your life."

He stared at her for a long moment. "You know, I think that's why I came here."

"I don't understand."

"I think...." he hesitated, then pushed ahead. "I just had a frustrating conversation with my dad, and I took a walk to try to shake it off. And I ended up here, I think because I knew you would understand."

Lizzy tried to wrap her brain around this. He'd come to talk to her? Specifically?

"So...you don't want to order anything," she clarified.

A small smile graced his lips as he chuckled. "Got a recommendation?"

"Hm." She brought a finger to her lips as she pretended to consider it. "The peanut butter and anchovy smoothie is pretty hot right now."

"Oh, God." His bark of laughter, which was instantaneous, was followed by a heart stopping grin. "Please don't make me drink that."

"Are you sure?" She grinned back. "It's a little salty, a little sweet...Mostly salty."

"That sounds...gross. Also, are you trying to tell me you're mad at me?"

He surprised a laugh out of her.

"Yes." When his eyes widened she continued with an impish smile, "It is gross—and it smells worse than you think. And no, I'm not mad at you."

Relieved, his eyes danced when he returned the smile. "Good."

"Lizzy!" From the back, Charlotte's voice rang through the kitchen, getting progressively louder as she made her way to the front. "You'll never guess what came in the mail!"

She came to a halt when she made it to the front, saw Will at the counter.

"Oh, I'm sorry, I didn't realize we had a customer."

But Lizzy eyed the padded envelope in Charlotte's hands. "Is that what I think it is?"

Smiling, Charlotte nodded.

Beaming, Lizzy turned back to Will. "Sorry, Will, did you decide on anything?"

He shook his head, enjoying her excitement. "Go ahead and open it. I know you want to."

She didn't hesitate to turn back to Charlotte, who handed her the envelope. Right there on the lip of the envelope was the Brown insignia, and her heart caught in her throat.

"This is the one I wanted," she whispered, tearing up a little as she looked at Charlotte. "Dad's alma mater."

"Open it, honey," Charlotte said, her voice soft but encouraging.

"What if it says I didn't get in?"

"It doesn't," Will cut in, and Lizzy hastily blinked the coming tears away before looking at him. Out of the corner of her eye, she could tell Charlotte was appraising him.

"How do you know?" Lizzy asked.

"Because it's a thick manila envelope," he chuckled, and her shoulders loosened a bit as she understood what he was saying. "They don't send rejection letters in those."

"Right." But embarrassment gave way to elation, and she couldn't wait any longer. She ripped open the envelope, pulled out the stack of papers inside, and skipping over the Brown letterhead at the top, directed her glistening eyes to the line on the first page starting with *Dear Elizabeth*. "I got in. I got in to Brown."

Throwing professionalism aside, Charlotte hugged her tight. "I knew you could do it."

"Brown, huh?" Will grinned. "That's my top pick, too."

"Really?" In her euphoria, Lizzy didn't realize how big her smile was when she looked at him. "Did you get in, or did you not get a letter yet?"

He nodded. "I got in."

"Cool."

"Well, well." Charlotte watched the pair with a sly smile. "Lizzy, you didn't tell me you had a new friend. Are you going to introduce me?"

Lizzy's cheeks flushed with a faint rosy hue. "Oh, we're not..."

"I'm Will Darcy." He held out a hand to Charlotte over the counter.

"I'm Charlotte Lucas, the manager of this establishment." Charlotte shook his hand, brisk and businesslike, then softened. "I've seen you in here before, haven't I?"

"This is not my first visit," Will confirmed. Then as he eyed the envelope still in Lizzy's hands, something seemed to occur to him, and he tilted his head at her. "Wait, did you have your mail sent here?"

So he'd noticed. Well, he knew how things were with Frances, or at least some of it. And for some reason, it was easier to talk to him about it than it was to those closer to her; likely because he was outside it. She could talk to Closet Poet about it too, of course, but he didn't know the people involved.

Charlotte looked like she was about to jump in, so Lizzy answered, "No. I put Charlotte's address on all my college applications."

As it dawned on him, his brows rose, and he tipped his head. "Because of Frances?"

Lizzy nodded. "I don't trust her not to go through my mail. Or toss my acceptance letters without my ever seeing them."

"I know you said..." he trailed of, shook his head. "But why would she do that?"

Lizzy shrugged. "To keep me dependent on her. Keep me working here for minimum wage, working for free at the house. Never mind that I could find a new job and live somewhere else."

"Why don't you?"

She wasn't expecting the question, and it unsettled her. It was something she'd asked herself before, but pushed to the back of her mind because she wasn't ready to consider it.

Charlotte echoed the question by giving her a pointed look. "You know you could come stay with me."

Lizzy sighed. "I will. After graduation."

Charlotte looked like she wanted to protest, but Lizzy set her papers down behind the counter and turned back to Will before she could say anything further. "So. What'll it be?"

"Uh." Will's eyes shifted between her and Charlotte, but whatever he was thinking, he set it aside. "Just a black coffee, please."

"Okey dokey," she said with forced cheer. She poured his coffee into a to-go cup, pressed the lid on while Charlotte rang him up. When she held the cup out to him, he took it slowly, searching her eyes with his own, as if checking to see she was okay.

Finally, he pulled away, nodded to her and Charlotte.

"Have a good day, Will," Charlotte said, the small twist of her lips telling Lizzy she thought there was something going on between them.

"You, too." When Will got to the door, he paused, looked back. "Thanks, Lizzy."

When he was gone, Lizzy released the breath she'd been holding. She wasn't entirely sure what he'd thanked her for, but she suspected it wasn't the coffee. And she wasn't sure how she felt about that. About him.

It had been pleasant to see him. It had felt like a little pick-me-up when he'd walked in. And she couldn't get the way he'd stared at her out of her mind. The way his eyes had burned into her.

She knew he was concerned about her, understood he'd already come to consider her a friend. But why? What was in it for him?

Unless he was playing her.

But no—Will was too honest for that. Honest to a fault, even. He'd implied he liked spending time with her, so she had to trust he meant it. That didn't keep her from being skeptical, though.

Or maybe, she had to admit, she was looking for reasons to be skeptical. Because on some level—a deep, long ignored level—she also had to acknowledge she was attracted to him.

Who wouldn't be?

It would be easy to run away with those feelings. To let attraction become something more. And it would be a mistake—because what would Will Darcy want with Lizzy Bennet?

And she couldn't forget Closet Poet.

"Well." Charlotte's smile was smug and knowing when Lizzy looked at her. "What was that you were saying last time, about him not flirting with you?"

"He wasn't," she insisted. "Isn't."

"Mm hm."

"We're just..." Acquaintances? Classmates? "Friends. Kind of."

That trademark pointed look returned. "You told him about Frances."

"I kind of had to, a little. His best friend is dating Jane, so they've been sitting with us at lunch, and we were assigned to a project together, so we've had to spend even more time together," she explained. "It was kind of inevitable he'd find out something about my home life."

"But you told him."

She sighed. "Yes, I've talked to him about it."

Charlotte smiled softly, then reached out to run a hand over Lizzy's hair. "What's holding you back, baby? I don't just mean with that boy, I mean everything. You said it yourself—you could move in with me, find a new job—or instead, just enjoy what's left of your senior year. Be a teenager for once. It's hard for us here, knowing you've had to grow up too fast, watching you be so stoic."

Lizzy felt tears well up again, but dug for that stoicism to keep them at bay. "I...It's just not time. I don't know how to explain, but I just don't think it's time yet."

"Is there a right time?" Charlotte asked. "I know this place means a lot to you, and that house is the only home you know, but whether it's now or six months from now won't change how you feel about it."

Maybe. But right now she was feeling like she didn't want to face that until she had to.

"If only she hadn't gotten everything," she said instead. "Sometimes I can't help but be mad at him, for not leaving a will. Maybe he would've left everything to her anyway, but I can't help thinking things would be different."

"You know, I've always wondered about that." Charlotte murmured.

"What do you mean?"

She paused, then said, "Not long after your dad and Frances married, he told me he was having a will drawn up. He asked me to be his executor."

"He did?" This was news to Lizzy. "Why didn't you ever say anything?"

"Because I didn't want to upset you further. When nothing came of it, when no will was found, I assumed he hadn't gotten it done in time."

"And...now you don't think that?"

Charlotte stared at the counter, lost in her thoughts, and likely some memory Lizzy had no inkling of. "I don't know."

A shiver ran down Lizzy's spine. Was it possible? All this time, could there have been a will somewhere?

Even if there was, Lizzy figured, it probably didn't matter now. In just over six months, she'd be out from under France's thumb; and a year from now, she thought as she looked at her Brown welcome packet, she'd be living a whole new life.

Twelve

THE REST of the weekend went by in a finger snap, and before he knew it, Will found himself sitting across from Lizzy at lunch. He thought, after the end of their conversation the other day, she'd be reluctant to talk to him, or be a little distant. But she smiled when he sat down, leaned an elbow on the table.

"So. Brown, huh?"

"Yeah," he said, frowning.

Her brow quirked. "You don't seem terribly excited about it."

"The problem is telling my dad that's where I want to go," he admitted. "He wants me to go to Stanford."

"Why?"

He shrugged. "It's his dream that I play football there, and study accounting, and then take over the family business eventually. He's even got some scout or something coming to the game on Friday."

"Wow. No pressure."

"Tell me about it." He didn't want to talk about himself, or his dad. He wanted to talk about her. "So, Brown for you, too?"

"Oh." Though she seemed surprised by the abrupt turn in

conversation, she took it in stride. "Yeah...that's where my dad went. I've always wanted to go there."

He grinned. "And now you can."

The corner of her mouth turned up. "Now I can."

"Why did you have your letters sent to Charlotte? Instead of Jane, I mean."

Her smile was sadder, more wistful now. "Charlotte was my mom's best friend. She's...well, she's the only mother I've ever really had."

"Then I'm glad you have her."

"Me, too." But she said it absently, like her mind was no longer really on the conversation.

Following the direction of her gaze, he looked around the courtyard at all the people staring at them. And, thinking of their conversation from Friday, he leaned forward over the table, like he had a secret to share. When her eyes refocused on him, he looked right into them and said in a solemn tone, "Quack."

For a split second she blinked, then a surprised, delighted laugh sputtered out of her.

"Quack?" she asked with a knowing arch of her eyebrow.

His lips curved, and he nodded. "Quack quack."

Leaning back, she smiled more fully before nodding back, like they'd just struck a deal. "Quack."

He was sure they were both grinning like idiots; let's see what they have to say about *that*, he thought.

As Charlie and Jane approached the table and sat down, Charlie took in their expressions. "What did we miss?"

Lizzy shrugged. "Will was just reminding me how to be impervious to gossip."

"Oh, there's a trick to that, is there?" Charlie asked, smirking.

"Mostly it has to do with not caring what others think of you,"

Will said. "Elizabeth knows how to do that, she just needed a little push."

"Is there gossip about Lizzy?" Jane asked, concern etching her brow.

Anne, who'd approached the table with Ricky as Jane spoke, shrugged as she sat down. "Mostly it's just speculation. A lot of people have seen you together, but not like, *together*, so they're even more curious."

"Why my relationship status is of such importance, I'll never understand," Will muttered.

"Cuz you're the prime rib, bro." Ricky lightly punched Will on the shoulder. "Most people aren't going to make a move on you unless they think you're single."

Will sighed. "Can we change the subject please?"

"Well..." Anne bit her lips, looked at Lizzy.

"What?" Lizzy asked, glancing around.

"It's just, there's this guy," Anne said, meeting Lizzy's gaze. "I don't know his name, but he likes to wear bowties. He went up to Caroline and Louisa on Friday, after you and Will left school together. I was nearby with my friend Jenny, and we overheard him say some weird stuff about how he'd asked you out, but you turned him down because you thought you could turn Will's head instead."

She paused, her face scrunching up a little. "Those were the words he used. 'Turn Will's head.'"

"Colin." Lizzy grit her teeth.

Will was surprised to hear Anne talk so much in one sitting. He was sure not having Caroline and Louisa around to talk over her helped, but he also suspected Jane's cheery calm and Lizzy's openness had something to do with it. He'd heard her mention her friend Jenny—a fellow cheerleader—before, but this was the first time he caught the blush on her cheeks when she said her name.

"What did Caroline say?" he asked.

Anne shrugged again. "She suspected something like that, but mostly she just thought he was weird and wanted him to go away."

Lizzy's shoulders sagged a little. "I wonder if that's why people have been staring at me."

"People tend to stare at whatever table Will is at," Ricky said, his mouth half full of Takis.

It seemed the whole table had gotten in on the snack deal.

"The fact that this is basically our usual group has only added to that, I'd think," Charlie added.

"Definitely," Ricky agreed. "It's just like old times, except we traded two snobby girls for two nice ones."

Was he implying that this table was now the quote unquote "popular" table? And that Lizzy and Jane were unquestionably a part of it? Will watched Lizzy and Jane exchange a look, as if they were wondering the same thing.

Then Lizzy blinked, and muttered, "Meanwhile, in an alternate universe..."

"Sounds like I need to have a word with this Colin guy after all." Will tilted his head. "Has he bothered you again?"

"No, he hasn't." Lizzy folded her arms. "And no, you don't need to talk to him. I told you, you'll just make it worse."

Will shook his head. "And I told you, when I tell people to back off, they usually do."

"*Usually* being the key word. Colin is a little socially inept." She leaned forward to meet his eyes. "Promise me you won't talk to him about this."

"No can do."

She gave him a pointed look, one that reminded him of the one his mother used to give him when he was being stubborn.

"I thought we were friends now."

If she thought that would get him to back down, she had

another thing coming. "Exactly. We're friends, and I do what I can to protect my friends."

"He does," Charlie confirmed. "And unless you can convince him he's wrong, he'll do it anyway."

When Lizzy looked like she was going to protest, like she had the argument that would convince him, he held up a hand to forestall her. "How about this? I won't seek him out, but if he approaches me, I won't hold back from setting him straight."

She huffed. "Do you always think your way is best?"

He just stared her down, and finally she rolled her eyes.

"Fine. If he seeks you out, say whatever you want."

His smile was small, but victorious nonetheless. "Thank you."

He felt eyes on the back of his neck, and instinctively, he turned his head to look at the fountain table.

Caroline had been glaring, but she perked up when he looked over, sent him a sultry smile accompanied by a little wave of her fingers. Ignoring her, he turned back to his friends.

Sooner or later, he'd probably have to deal with her again, too.

When Will pulled up to the café after practice, Lizzy was already waiting outside, leaning against the brick exterior.

They'd agreed to meet up again to work on their paper, but this time he'd convinced her to come over to his house instead of going to the library. It would be approaching dinner time, he pointed out, and she could get a delicious home cooked meal she didn't cook herself.

He could just imagine Mrs. R fretting over Lizzy. And he just knew Gianna would love her.

Lizzy was staring at her phone, bottom lip caught between her teeth as if she were contemplating the end of the world. For all he knew she was—or, the end of her world at least.

She looked up when he pulled up to the curb, gave him a small, distracted smile before pushing off the wall.

"How was work?" he asked her when she'd settled into the passenger seat.

She shrugged. "Same job, different day."

"Exciting."

"Isn't it just?" When he lifted a brow at her sarcastic tone, she deflated and rubbed at her eyes. "Sorry, I'm...tired."

"And cranky. Do you not drink your own coffee?"

That got a small laugh out of her. "I do. I made myself a lavender latte. But I guess I meant I'm mentally tired, not physically."

"Ah. Good thing we're about to go do a bunch of thinking then," he pointed out.

"I'll be fine. If I'm thinking about academics, I won't be over-thinking the rest of my life."

"Fair enough."

Before long, he pulled into the driveway of his house. He watched Lizzy as she took it in, got out of the car slowly.

"This is your house?"

She sounded impressed, but also a bit overwhelmed.

"Yeah..." He turned to the sprawling, immaculate mansion, with its doric columns and creeping ivy, wide second floor balcony, and four car garage.

She said nothing more as he led her inside, through the front door. Her eyes skimmed over everything as he showed her a few rooms, like the living room, the music room, and where the bathroom was. The more she saw, the more she seemed to loosen up.

"You seem surprised," he commented.

"Well, the outside is nice," she said, a little sheepishly, "but it's also kind of intimidating. The inside is a bit more upscale than I'm used to, but it still has that lived-in feel. It's easier to relax knowing this is a home."

"Why wouldn't it be a home?"

"Ah..."

She didn't really have a chance to respond, as he'd led her to the kitchen, where Mrs. R stood at the stove, mixing something heavenly with a wooden spoon.

"Will! Just in time," she said as they entered, her smile everything warm and welcoming. "You must be Will's friend."

Will was glad he and Elizabeth had established they were indeed friends, or this moment might be supremely awkward.

"Hi, I'm Lizzy Bennet." Elizabeth held out her hand to shake Mrs. R's, and Will noted the approving smile Mrs. R gave her as she took it.

"It's nice to meet you, dear," she said in her I'm-going-to-mother-hen-you way. "I'm Mrs. Reynolds, the housekeeper here."

Elizabeth's eyes widened. "You take care of this *whole* house? But it's huge."

A deep, braying laughter escaped Mrs. R's lips. "Oh, no. I mostly do the cooking around here. I do some basic cleaning and tidying up, but I get a cleaning service in for any major things. And there's a gardener for all the landscaping."

Mrs. R was more than a housekeeper. He'd lost count of the scraped knees she'd patched up, torn clothing she'd stitched, and homework she'd helped with over the years. Not to mention her attendance at so many of his and Gianna's concerts and games. He was about to add his two cents when a blonde ball of energy barreled into the kitchen and nearly tackled him.

He caught his sister as she squealed, "Will, you're home!"

"How much sugar have you had today?" he asked, hugging her

back, then pulling back to examine her with an exaggerated expression.

Gianna just stuck out her tongue at him, then perked up when she noticed they had a guest.

"Hi, I'm Georgianna, but mostly everyone calls me Gianna for short. Georgianna is an aggressively long name."

"I think she meant egregiously," Will supplied. Gianna stuck out her tongue again.

Elizabeth's amusement was palpable, her eyes dancing merrily as she said, "You Darcys and your use of four-syllable words."

"We do appreciate a good vocabulary."

Still smiling, Elizabeth addressed Gianna. "I'm Elizabeth, but most people call me Lizzy."

"It's nice to meet you, Lizzy. I'm so glad Will finally brought a girl home!"

That seemed to put a hitch in Lizzy's stride. "Well, uh..."

"Dinner will be ready in a moment," Mrs. R cut in. "Will you be joining us, Lizzy, or do you and Will have to get started on your project?"

"Oh." Lizzy tapped her foot a little, shot him a glance. "I don't—"

"We'll eat first," Will interjected. "I'm starving. No use trying to get work done on an empty stomach."

Mrs. R nodded like she'd expected this. "Set the table for four, then."

"No dad?" Gianna asked, deflating a little.

"He called to say he had to work late." Will didn't miss the disapproval in Mrs. R's tone, and he suspected Lizzy caught it as well. "I'll make up a bowl to leave for him."

As Will pulled down bowls and plates, gathered silverware, the oven timer beeped loudly; Mrs. R slipped on an oven mitt and pulled out a sheet lined with a dozen freshly baked biscuits. She set them aside before turning off the flame under the pot.

The four of them had a homey, companionable meal of Mrs. R's homemade chicken and wild rice soup, and flaky, buttery biscuits. Mrs. R asked them a lot about school when she realized Lizzy hedged around questions about her family, diplomatically changing the subject.

Gianna wasn't as subtle.

"Do you have any siblings, Lizzy? How old are they?" she asked, and Will surmised she was hoping Lizzy had siblings closer to her age.

Lizzy paused before answering carefully. "I have two stepsisters, who're both juniors, and a best friend who's like a sister. She's a senior, too."

"Oh." Gianna was disappointed, but quickly recovered. "Will said he had to pick you up from work. Where do you work?"

"Frances's. It's a café."

Will noted she didn't mention it was her family's business.

Gianna scrunched her nose. "The weird, pink frilly place?"

"*Gianna*," Will warned.

"It's okay," Lizzy assured them, a slight smile revealing her amusement. "It is weird, and pink and frilly."

Mrs. R tactfully changed the subject again, and Will sent her a grateful look across the table, though it soon shifted to a look of mild horror when Gianna started talking about a boy she had a crush on at school.

When they'd finished their meal, Mrs. R roped Gianna into helping her clear the table, and ushered he and Lizzy out with a little shooing motion and a smile.

"Follow me," Will gestured down the hall, and Lizzy followed. "You're going to love this."

"Oh?" She raised a brow. "And why is that?"

"You'll see."

She was quiet. He didn't expect her to be talkative, but she seemed even more pensive than usual, and he tilted his head at her as they neared the door he was leading her to.

"What?" she asked, giving him a pointed look.

"Something on your mind?" he asked.

"No." She shrugged. "I was just thinking how nice it is to see how close you and your sister are with Mrs. Reynolds. She seems very...motherly."

He nodded. "She's the only mother figure we've had for some time now. I guess you could say Mrs. R is to us what Charlotte is to you."

The small smile she gave him was one of unequivocal understanding. "Does Gianna remember your mother much?"

"No. Mrs. R and I try to tell her things sometimes."

"I was pretty young, too. Five or six, I think. I have a few memories, and some things my dad told me, but the rest come from Charlotte and the others at the café."

"My dad rarely talks about her." His shoulders tensed. "He shut down after she died. And he didn't really come back, not all the way. Sometimes it feels like I lost him, too."

He frowned, playing back what he'd said as they stopped in front of the door, his eyes widening as he turned to her. "I'm sorry, I didn't think—"

"It's fine." There was that understanding smile again, this time laced with sadness. "I know what you meant."

"Do you mind if I asked how they died?"

"I suppose not." Her eyes drifted down the hall, distant and unseeing. "Breast cancer for mom, car accident for dad."

"I'm sorry." He didn't know what else to say, and guilt hit him as he felt intrusive for asking, so he offered up his own tragedy. "It was ovarian cancer for my mom."

She looked back at him now, nodded. Then she looked expectantly at the wide mahogany door they stood in front of. "I think that's enough melancholy for today."

"Agreed." He turned the handle, opened the door, and gestured for her to enter ahead of him. Since he went in immediately after, he caught the soft gasp that left her lips as she realized what the room was.

Every wall was covered in floor-to-ceiling oak shelves, thick and sturdy enough to hold endless stacks and rows of books—and a few collector's items here and there. In the center of the room was a coffee-colored leather couch, opposite a pair of sea green wingback chairs. Between them was a glass coffee table.

"You have a library." Lizzy breathed out, the awe lighting up her sparkling blue eyes. "An honest-to-God library."

"It's the work of many generations," he informed her, and she turned, regarding him with a mixture of that same awe, and some disbelief.

"You even have a rolling ladder."

"What library would be complete without a rolling ladder?"

She eyed it longingly, and he smirked. "Do you want to ride it? I'll push you," he offered when she only stared at him.

Then, she bit her lip, and he knew she was dying to do it.

"C'mon." He tugged her bag off her shoulder, set it on the floor next to the coffee table, where his backpack already sat. Then he gently pulled her arm, guided her toward the ladder.

She pursed her lips at his high-handedness, but put up no resistance. He dropped her arm when they stopped in front of the ladder, gripped the handle on the side.

"Up you go."

She tried and failed to keep a straight face. Gripping the other handle, she scampered up a few steps, then turned slightly to lean a hip against one. Still gripping the handle with one hand, she looped an arm through a rung. "I'm ready."

He pushed, slowly at first to allow her to get used to it. The ladder's track went all the way around the room, so he figured she should be treated to the whole ride. He slowed for the corners, but picked up speed in between, and she let out a laughing whoop, eventually bracing herself to lean out, one hand trailing along the books as they went by.

Like Belle in *Beauty and the Beast*, he thought.

"That was a trip." A little breathless, Lizzy hopped down. "I feel like Belle in the opening of *Beauty and the Beast*."

"I was just thinking that."

"Were you?"

"I was."

"Huh." Her eyes were as merry as her teasing smile. "I didn't take you for a Disney connoisseur."

"I have a little sister," he pointed out.

"Fair," she conceded.

Without either of them realizing it, the moment stretched on, quiet but charged as they stared smiling at each other. He was drawn in by her eyes, those sparkling blue-violet pools; it was a bit like being in a haze. He took an unconscious step forward.

And the spell snapped.

Elizabeth blinked, her smile dipping a bit before turning into one of self-consciousness. His own haze cleared.

"Shall we?" He gestured to the coffee table.

"Yes." She turned and walked briskly to the couch, though she tried to make it look like she wasn't in a hurry. She also wasted no time pulling out her books and laptop.

They spent the rest of the evening working diligently on their paper—perhaps a little too diligently. If he even hinted at speaking of something personal, she redirected the conversation back to their work.

He managed to convince her to let him drive her home, but she was mostly silent during the ride as well. The exception was when she suggested they establish their next meetup ahead of time. He agreed, and they settled on Thursday; when he suggested his house again, she hesitated, but when she couldn't think of a good excuse to refuse, she capitulated.

He understood she'd rather go to the library. It was her sanctuary. Safe. And his home was a new experience—not to mention large, and probably, as she'd mentioned, a little intimidating. But it was still, as she'd acknowledged herself, a home that was indeed lived in. He wanted her to feel it.

She likely had, for a little while, anyway.

"Thanks for the ride," she said when he stopped at the curb outside her house.

"You're welcome. Anytime."

She gathered up her bag, a small laugh escaping her. "You mean you're not put off by the creepy gnome army?"

"The gnomes are a little weird, I'll give you that." He chuckled.

"Would it be weirder if I told you I've named them all?"

"Named them? Why?"

"To make them less creepy." She counted off on her fingers. "There's Sven, Wilhelm, Eugene, Rodney, Benjamina, Mr. Potato Head, The Undertaker—"

"Wait, wait," he interrupted, bursting out laughing. "You thought naming one after one of the creepiest professional wrestlers would make it less creepy?"

"The Undertaker's a badass." She shrugged, barely holding in her own laughter. "Also, he just looks like The Undertaker to me."

"Well, now I have to meet him."

Her smile immediately dimmed. "Some other time."

"Sure," he said, like the mood hadn't changed. "But anyway, the house itself is pretty picturesque, and so are the rosebushes."

"My mom grew them," Elizabeth said, her voice barely above a whisper. "Thankfully, neither me or my dad mentioned that to Frances; she probably would have ripped them out, otherwise."

The cold-hearted witch, he thought, even as he rejoiced Lizzy had spoken of something personal.

Then, as if she just realized what she'd said, she straightened and opened the door to climb out. "Thanks again," she said quickly.

"See you tomorrow."

"See you."

He watched her power-walk up the drive to the front door. She wasn't running away, exactly, but she was definitely avoiding something. Something to do with him.

Maybe it was about time to take off the mask.

Thirteen

HER PHONE LIT up like a beacon. She hadn't spoken to Closet Poet in days, and she couldn't decide if she was relieved or annoyed to hear from him.

Then again, she hadn't reached out to him, either.

She picked up her phone, bit her lip.

> Hey, yourself.

Ugh, did that sound too flirty? She'd thought it just the right combination of I missed you/where have you been, but now she wasn't so sure.

> I'm sorry I haven't messaged. I guess you could say I've been preoccupied.

> It's okay. So have I.

143

He must have known what he wanted to say, because he was quick to reply.

I've been thinking a lot about our situation.

Oh, boy, that didn't sound good. Maybe he'd decided he didn't want to be with her after all, and was messaging to break it off once and for all. Even as she acknowledged it would be easier that way, her heart sank.

I think we've put it off long enough.

She swallowed, waiting for the blow.

We need to meet for real. Soon.

She hadn't realized she'd been holding her breath until it rushed out of her with an audible *whoosh*. He still wanted to meet her.

You're right. How soon?

This weekend? I've got a pretty busy week.

So did she, but she could make Saturday or Sunday work.

Works for me.

Good. I can't wait to give you your bracelet back.

She gasped. How had she forgotten about the bracelet? Then another thought hit her, and she braced herself to ask him about it.

> Is that the only reason you want to meet me? To give my bracelet back?

No.

She sighed with relief, and a moment later, another message popped up.

> I'd be lying if I said I didn't want to kiss you again.

He was really putting her heart through the wringer—from nervy disappointment to elation in a heartbeat. But he wasn't done.

> I want, as myself, to kiss you, as you. No masks. Just us.

She'd be lying, too, if she said she didn't want that. A part of her wondered what would have happened if they'd just met that way the first time. They probably could have saved themselves this confusion.

Hindsight was a real Captain Obvious sometimes.

I want that, too.

Even as she sent it, she remembered the kiss they'd shared at the dance. The intensity in his eyes, so distinctly green even in only the glow of the courtyard lighting. And in the next second, those eyes belonged to Will Darcy, and she was remembering the way he'd looked at her when she'd stepped off the ladder in his library.

Her heart pounded.

It couldn't be, could it? No. She didn't think of Will that way. And there was certainly no way he'd ever think of her that way.

Right?

Right, she told herself firmly, and readied herself for bed.

But sleep was slow in coming. And when at last she did drift off, she dreamed she as Cinderella danced with Closet Poet under the spinning disco ball, the edges of the dance floor gauzy with warm, gossamer light. He wore the same pristine green Prince Charming outfit as he had before, and they whirled, whirled, whirled around the dance floor, seemingly floating as they smiled and gazed into each other's eyes, like lovers in a musical.

And as they whirled, their masks faded away. He no longer wore the powdered wig, and gazing back at her was Will. They continued to glide across the floor, one of his hands in hers, the other at the small of her back, while her palm rested against his shoulder. Slowly, magically, he tugged her a little closer, dipping his head down, and she automatically tipped her face up in invitation.

Elizabeth, he breathed, before his lips captured hers, and butterflies came to life inside her.

When she woke, groggy and confused, she could have sworn the shimmer of magic sparkles fell from her eyes as she rubbed them. She only vaguely remembered the dream, remembered she'd been dancing. She knew it had been a good dream—a very good dream, if the glowy feeling she'd woken with was anything to go by.

She was missing something important. It was there, on the edge of her consciousness, and her mind started to pick at the film covering it.

"LIZZY!"

A sudden banging on her bedroom door jolted her fully awake, and she scowled at the door.

"Get up and make me breakfast!" Lydia demanded.

Gritting her teeth, Lizzy sat up. A glance at the clock told her she'd slept half an hour past her usual wake up time. She must have slept through her alarm.

"Coming," she called, and rolled out of bed.

Dream forgotten, she readied for the day.

To Lizzy, the week seemed to crawl by. She'd been a tad sluggish on Tuesday, only righted by an extra cup of coffee. She still spent the day in a funk because she couldn't escape the feeling she was missing something.

Tuesday blended together with the first half of Wednesday. Wednesday afternoon only stood out because Will had made good on his threat—er, promise—to chew out Colin if he was approached.

Which, of course he was. Colin was as obtuse as it came.

Or perhaps *addressed* was a more appropriate word.

She witnessed the whole scene because she'd been on her way to Will's locker before AP Lit, only to see Colin amble over to him. Her instinct was to intercept him, but she held back.

A deal was a deal.

Plus, it might be satisfying to watch.

"Darcy, I must speak with you."

From where she stood, Lizzy could see Will's face just above Colin's head. He raised a brow and smirked slowly, like he was preparing for a set down. "Must you?"

"Indeed. I fear your stellar reputation is in danger. There are rumors about you and your relationship with Elizabeth Bennet."

"I'm aware." Will appeared aloof as he considered Colin, but Lizzy could tell he wanted to tear him a new one. "Fortunately, none of those rumors particularly bother me. And if they don't concern me, they shouldn't concern you, either."

"But I've seen it with my own eyes! She's turned your head."

"What?" Will snapped.

"Elizabeth." Colin clarified. "I know you wouldn't do Caroline the disservice, but if you're not careful, you could be lured in by Elizabeth's charms."

A mixture of confusion and exasperation suffused Will's face. "What in the ever-loving hell are you talking about? What's between me and Elizabeth is no one's business, especially not yours, or Caroline's."

"But—"

"I don't even like Caroline. And Lizzy doesn't like you—she's just too nice to tell you that. But I'm not."

"She's just playing hard to get," Colin insisted. "She knows she's not good enough for you."

Will's glare was full force fury in an instant, but his voice was deceptively calm. "If you ask me, 'hard to get' is something some asshole made up because the woman he wanted refused him, and he didn't know how to take no for an answer, so he used it as an excuse to keep pestering her."

Lizzy chuckled to herself. He was going to scare the crap out of Gianna's future boyfriends. Also, she'd never thought of it before, but he might be onto something with that 'hard to get' origin story.

Will stepped closer to Colin, towering over him like a storm cloud, snapping with lightning. "Let's get a couple things straight. When a woman says no, you listen. Period."

Colin was quaking too hard to respond, so Will continued, "And *you're* the one who isn't good enough for *her*. Your values are skewed—I suggest you straighten them out before you try asking someone else out. And since you seem to be the source of some of the baseless rumors about her, I'll thank you to stop spreading them."

When Colin only continued to quiver, Will eyed him and stepped back. "If I hear any more nonsense from you where Elizabeth is concerned, I will make your life miserable. Is that clear?"

Colin's head bobbed up and down with such rapidity, Lizzy thought he'd give himself whiplash.

"Good. Now get out of my sight."

With the haste of a runner off the starting block, Colin scrambled away. And with his focus no longer on the absurd conversation, Will's eyes caught hers.

She barely noticed the magnetism that drew her in as she stepped up to him, arched a brow. "Satisfied?"

He blew out a breath. "Annoyed. Maybe I'll feel the satisfaction later."

"He seems to have that effect on people."

He tilted his head. "Thanks for not interrupting."

She shrugged. "We made a deal."

"So we did."

"Hopefully you're right, and that's the end of it."

"It will be if he knows what's good for him."

They'd walked to class together, and drawn not a few eyes. Neither Will nor Colin had moderated their voices, so the gossip mill likely had some fresh water to churn, but for the first time, Lizzy didn't mind.

It wasn't until later she realized no one had stood up for her like that before. Usually she made it a point to stand up for herself, but it hadn't been too much of a hardship to step back and let Will handle it. The fact it was Will of all people who had done so surprised her, but it wasn't unwelcome.

She was, she admitted begrudgingly, a little bit grateful.

And for a moment, something pricked at her memory. The remnants of a dream. But then Mr. Goulding started class, and it was gone.

Fourteen

Thursday afternoon, Jane drove Lizzy to the Darcy home after work as they'd planned. Will had tried insisting on picking her up again, but Lizzy had tried to insist on walking. Jane didn't have plans with Charlie, so she'd suggested the alternative; since Lizzy hadn't spent as much quality time with her friend since she'd starting seeing Charlie, she jumped at the chance to ride with Jane instead.

Will couldn't argue with that.

Now she just had to make it through another evening at his house. Though she'd enjoyed her last visit, Lizzy would have preferred the public library. It was a gorgeous house, well maintained but still obviously lived in.

And huge.

It was a little uncomfortable to be reminded of the stock the Darcys came from. Her family wasn't poor, but her life was still a world away from his. It was probably good to remind herself of that. Plus, it just felt so...personal. He was more himself in his home, as anyone would be, and she wasn't sure how she felt about it yet.

She rang the bell and waited, surprised when the door opened after only a few seconds.

"Hey," said Will, ushering her inside. He seemed a little harried, but she wasn't sure if she should ask about it.

"Hey."

"Library good again? Want anything to drink before we start?"

"Not right now. Thank you."

He nodded, and though he smiled, it was a little strained. This seemed more like the Will she thought she knew—the one who spent most of his time scowling into the abyss—and it surprised her to realize it pained her to see his return.

She followed him down the hall toward the library, and as they neared the library door, a tall man with dark blonde hair stepped out of the kitchen. Upon spotting them, he sauntered toward them.

When Will stiffened, she figured this must be the infamous Robert Darcy.

"Well, hello," he said as he approached, giving her a charming, practiced smile. It was a friendly enough smile, but it also reminded her of the kind of charm businessmen put on in order to schmooze clients. "I didn't know we were going to have a guest today."

"Dad, this is Elizabeth. Elizabeth, this is my dad. Elizabeth and I are working on a paper for AP Lit," Will explained in a bland tone.

Robert held out his hand, and Elizabeth took it, shook firmly as she looked him in the eye. He seemed surprised by her directness, but pleased.

"Ah, an AP student. What is your paper about?"

Was he testing her? Or Will?

Or was he genuinely curious?

Either way, she tilted her head, curved her lips to one side. "A comparison of elements of the Prometheus myth to the story of Frankenstein. I suggested we call it 'Playing with Fire,' though our focus will be on the creation myth aspect."

"A double entendre." Robert nodded, understanding. "That's clever."

"I thought so."

"Tell me, Elizabeth, do you have a college picked out?" Robert asked.

"Dad."

"What?" Robert flicked a glance at his son's annoyed tone. "I can't ask about your friend's aspirations?"

"It's alright," Lizzy said, heading off Will's protest. "I just got accepted to Brown, which was my first choice."

"Impressive." Robert's smile seemed a little more genuine now, and she could hear the pride in his voice when he looked at Will. "Has Will here told you he's going to Stanford?"

She waited a beat. When no correction came, she side-eyed Will as she said, "He mentioned something about it."

"Great." Robert clapped Will on the shoulder. "Well, I'll let you get to work, then."

Will was silent as his father headed toward the stairs, but gestured for her to follow. She didn't bother asking what that was; he'd had an opportunity to tell his dad about Brown, and he hadn't.

To be fair, that probably wasn't a discussion he wanted to have with her around. He couldn't just be all "hey, actually I don't want to go to Stanford" and have that be the end of it, so now wasn't the time.

But she imagined his grim silence and casually expressionless face were his usual reaction to Robert's expectations.

To distract him, she tried putting his focus on something that always made him smile. "So, where's Gianna today?"

"She's at her violin lesson. And Mrs. R is visiting her daughter," he explained.

"Ah."

He already had a few things set up on the coffee table—laptop, textbook, notebook—so when he sat on the couch, she took a seat next to him, dropped her bag at her feet.

"Where do you want to start?" she asked, pulling out her own notebook and a pen.

They spent some time refining their thesis and marking particular passages they wanted to use. Lizzy noted down a few points they wanted to make in her notebook.

As she wrote, the ink in her pen got lighter and drier. She shook it, got a little more out of it, but was inevitably just scratching invisible lines into paper.

"Crap." She set the pen on the table, began digging around in her bag. She could have sworn she had another one.

"I've got one," Will offered.

He zipped open the front pocket of his backpack, pulled out a pen, held it out to her.

"Thanks." She turned her body and took it before looking up from their hands to his face.

Her breath hitched.

He was closer than she'd realized, his face inches from hers. He must have realized it too, because his expression shifted from questioning to something else she couldn't quite read. But she'd learned sometimes his eyes gave him away, so she looked right into them; he gazed back with an unwavering intensity that sent a swirl of tingles through her.

She was so mesmerized she almost didn't realize he was leaning closer, realize his intent, until his gaze broke for a moment to flick down to her lips. It took her another moment to realize she was leaning too—that Will Darcy was going to kiss her and she was inclined to kiss him back.

What would she tell Closet Poet?

The thought had her stiffening, pulling back just before Will's lips could brush hers. She and Closet Poet weren't technically together, but it wasn't fair to him. And it wasn't fair to Will, either.

"I...I can't."

She didn't miss the disappointment in those alluring green eyes, and she was surprised by the intensity of the regret that stung her heart.

"I'm sorry. I uh..." he cleared his throat. "Got distracted."

She couldn't think of anything to say in the face of such awkwardness, so she just nodded. "We should get back to it."

Deliberately, she held up the pen he'd given her.

"Right," he said, though more to himself than her. Then he practically lurched to his feet. "Do you want something to drink?"

"Sure." She tried to sound casual, but her voice sounded liked it'd pitched up a few octaves.

He nodded, and though he didn't run from the room, he did beat a hasty retreat.

Groaning, she leaned forward and knocked her forehead against the table a few times. She'd almost kissed Will Freaking Darcy; she'd *wanted* to, and she'd pulled away.

Was that nuts? That she'd pulled away in favor of a guy whose identity she didn't even know? A guy she'd barely spoken to the past week?

For a guy who'd been so eager to meet her in person, his hesitancy spoke volumes. Although, to be fair, her own hesitancy was probably hurting them both. They'd agreed to meet for real, but hadn't definitively established a time or place. It was time to end the back and forth once and for all.

Before she could rethink it, talk herself out of it, she whipped her phone out of her pocket, opened her messages to Closet Poet, and typed.

> Hey. So I was thinking about where we should meet, and I thought the public library might be good neutral ground. Thoughts?

Taking a deep breath, she sent the message.

On the table, Will's phone buzzed. She didn't think anything of it as she glanced at it—until she thought she saw the name Elizabeth on the screen.

But that could just be coincidence, right? Heart thudding wildly, her eyes zeroed in on Will's phone, now looking a little ominous.

Glancing at the door, she reached over to tap the screen, wake his phone up. But with her eyes watching the door more than her hand, her coordination was a little off—and instead of a phone, her fingers met the rough, scratchy material of Will's backpack.

In her haste to withdraw, her arm knocked it over, nearly sending it to the floor. Instead, the contents of the backpack's front pocket spilled out.

"Crap," Lizzy muttered, scrambling to her knees and moving to shove the small stockpile of writing implements back in the pouch. That's what she got for trying to snoop.

As she lifted the backpack, she froze.

There among the perfectly sharpened pencils and high-quality ball point pens was a sliver of gold. Brushing the utensils aside, her breath caught in the back of her throat, and she reached out, picked up a slim, gold bracelet interlaid with golden roses and tiny pearls.

Her bracelet.

The one she'd lost at the dance.

The one Closet Poet said he'd found.

Will was Closet Poet? Even while some part of her brain recognized it as truth, another part rebelled. There was just no way it was him, right?

Heart still pounding in her ears, she looked back down at her messages. Her thumb hovered over the call button next to Closet Poet's name, and she swallowed. Holding her breath, she pressed down.

Seconds after her phone sounded a dialing ring, Will's phone buzzed, the vibrations loud and jarring against the glass of the tabletop.

In a daze, she leaned over the table. Finally, she made herself look at the screen.

She thought maybe her heart had stopped beating, but she was proven wrong when nervous energy coursed through her.

Yep. It said Elizabeth, clear as day.

Not Lit Fairy. *Elizabeth.*

The phone stopped buzzing, and the screen dimmed, but she didn't move. Then, knees a little wobbly, she managed to stand.

She needed to pace this off.

There was no doubt now. Not only was Will Darcy Closet Poet, the guy she'd been pouring her heart out to, he also had already figured out she was Lit Fairy. How long had he known?

Oh, man. Was that why he'd suddenly started talking to her more? But that was...

That was right after the dance. The Monday after the dance.

And she'd been totally oblivious the whole time. He must think her incredibly stupid.

"So, we've got Dr. Pepper or La Croix," Will said as he returned to the room. "I took a guess you'd want a Dr. Pepper, so if..."

He trailed off when he saw her stop pacing to stand frozen. His eyes drifted to her phone in one hand, her bracelet in the other, then to his backpack with its partially spilled guts, and finally back up to her pale face and unmistakably pained expression.

"You...knew." It was barely above a whisper, but he heard it. "T-this whole time, you knew."

His shoulders sagged a little, but he met her eyes and nodded.

"Was it when Charlie asked Jane out? When you realized I was Cinderella?"

He took a deep breath, then admitted, "No. I realized at the dance."

"When you..." Her eyes widened, and she deliberately steadied her breath as her cheeks warmed. "When you kissed me?"

He nodded again. "I'd figured it out by then, yes."

She made a sound, something between a laugh and disbelief. "So this whole time, you've known it was me, and didn't bother to tell me? Why?"

"I told you why." He did his best to swallow through the lump in his throat. "I didn't think it would be fair if you knew that I knew. I'm sorry you found out this way. I was hoping..."

"What? You were hoping what? That you'd tell me and I'd just fall at the feet of Mr. Popular Will Darcy? Were you really afraid I'd be disappointed, or were you putting off telling me because you were afraid what everyone would think? Were you even going to tell me at all?"

She regretted the words as soon as they left her mouth. She'd seen for herself he wasn't what he let everyone believe.

His eyes narrowed, but he bit back whatever retort he was going to say and sighed, defeated. "No, *this* is what I was afraid of."

"This?"

"I knew you didn't like me," he said simply, but she heard the pain in his voice. "That Monday after the dance, I was going to tell you, and return your bracelet. But I overheard you when Jane suggested it could be me, and I couldn't do it. I mean, can you honestly say you would have been happy to find out who I was that day?"

Ashamed, she closed her eyes, squeezed them to fight off the sting of tears.

"I was afraid," he continued, "That even after trying to get to know you as myself, you'd still think I'm some spoiled, selfish rich kid."

Her eyes shot open. "I don't think that."

"Really? Because you seem disappointed."

"I'm sorry." Despite her best efforts, the tears brimmed, and a few escaped. "I'm in shock, I think. I...I don't know what I feel right now."

"I know. It's why I wanted to give you time. To accept it could be me," he clarified when she gave him a blank look. "Do you remember what I said about wearing a mask?"

She sniffled, quoted, "I don't have to wear a mask with you."

"When I heard what you said about me at school, I realized my mask had worked a little too well." He gave in to the urge to go to her, stepping to the coffee table and setting down the sodas. Then, straightening to look at her tear streaked face, he gently pulled her wrist toward him, carefully pried the bracelet out of her fingers. "The mask was all you could see of Will Darcy, and since you, thankfully, are *not* the type to fall at my feet because of who I am, I realized I had to let you see behind it before you could accept I was Closet Poet."

When he'd clasped the gold chain around her wrist, he met her shining blue eyes. "I wanted you to wonder on your own if it could be me. To want it to be me."

She wished she could tell him she did want it to be him, but she wasn't sure it was true. Maybe she'd been on her way to hoping it was him, but she didn't think she'd quite gotten there. Although, she had nearly just kissed him, thinking he was only Will.

The only thing that had stopped her was knowing it was unfair to both him and Closet Poet. She nearly scoffed at the irony.

"I think I was starting to hope it was you," she finally said, not meeting his eyes. Instead she bit her lip, played with the bracelet he'd so lovingly put on for her. "If only because I was so torn up at the idea of falling for you when there was someone else."

He closed his eyes like he was in pain. "I'm sorry. I didn't think about how that would make you feel."

"And how would *you* have felt, if I'd kissed you just now?" His head snapped up, and she continued, "Knowing I didn't know you and Closet Poet were the same person, but kissing you despite having feelings for him? That I would do that?"

"I wasn't planning on doing that." Will shook his head. "I had no intention of kissing you, or manipulating you, I just...wasn't thinking."

"Evidently not."

"I'm sorry," he repeated. "I should have told you sooner. I was just enjoying this time with you as myself; maybe it was selfish, but it was nice not to wear the mask."

She was quiet a moment, and he thought she was going to get angry again. But instead, when she looked at him, he saw sorrow in her eyes.

"Will, just because you dropped the mask with me doesn't mean you're not still wearing it."

"What do you mean?"

"Earlier, with your dad. You didn't contradict him."

Irritation sparked in his gut, and he spoke more sharply than he intended. "He doesn't have anything to do with this."

"Of course he does," she snapped back. "He's part of the reason for your mask."

"He expects me to just do what he wants without questioning it. It's easier to let him think I want what he wants."

"*Or*," she said, folding her arms. "Maybe he expects you to want what he wants because you haven't explicitly told him otherwise. It's possible he could accept you want something else, but you won't know if you don't tell him. Or were you just going to let Stanford tell him you didn't accept?"

"Maybe," he grumbled. "I considered it."

"You know that's not fair to him, or to you. He deserves to hear what you want from you, and you deserve to be able to tell him. Don't let this push you apart."

The fact she was right only irritated him more. It was his own fault, his own cowardice that had kept him from speaking up, and even in this area of his life it was haunting him. Though he knew he had no real excuse, he said, "It's not that simple."

"Isn't it?" she challenged.

"Well I don't see you taking your own advice," he shot back.

Her jaw dropped as her arms fell listlessly to her sides. "E-excuse you?"

"You heard me." He huffed, taking a moment to soften his tone, since he knew it was unfair of him to toss her advice back in her face. "I know your situation is different, but it doesn't mean you don't have a choice, Lizzy. You're a legal adult—you're not beholden to Frances anymore. And I know I'm not the only one who's pointed that out to you."

She sounded a little petulant when she said, "I know that."

"Do you?" he pushed. "The way that Frances treats you is

nothing short of emotional abuse, but instead of leaving, you still let her walk all over you and order you around."

"I'll be free of her when I graduate and go off to Brown." The argument sounded just as hollow as it had every other time she'd used it.

"You really want to wait that long? Seriously, what's the hold up?"

"What do you suggest I do?" She threw up her hands.

He gave her a look that said *I know you know*. "You suggested it yourself. Move in with Charlotte, and find a new job—or instead of getting a job, you could try out for the softball team."

"You make it sound so easy. To just leave my family's café, and the house I grew up in."

He shook his head. "I know it wouldn't be. But do you seriously think your dad would want you to stick around if he knew what your life was like?"

She blanched, and he immediately regretted the question.

"I'm sorry, I—"

"It's fine." She held up a hand. "I just never considered that."

Since he felt like he'd put his foot in his mouth enough, he stayed silent, waiting for her to say something instead. She looked down at their books and papers, finally putting her phone back in her pocket with a sigh.

"I should probably go."

"Lizzy—"

"No, I should go," she said more forcefully, looking back at him with tired eyes. "The fact is, you've had time to get used to this. I'm sorry to leave you in the lurch, but I need to process this."

"I...understand. Do you want me to drive you?"

"No, that's okay." She gathered her things, shoved them haphazardly into her messenger bag. He picked up one of the cans still on the table, held it out to her when she slung the bag over her shoulder.

"At least take the Dr. Pepper."

She allowed a small smile. "Thanks."

He watched her as she slid the can into her bag, went to the door. She paused when she reached it, turned back to him.

"I'll...I'll see you tomorrow," she said, then disappeared out the door, leaving him to wonder how everything had gone so awry.

Fifteen

THOUGHTS TUMBLED over each other in their haste to make their way to the front of Lizzy's mind. She practically power-walked away from Will's giant, fancy house, wanting to get away as fast as possible.

Maybe it was cowardly of her, but she'd meant it when she said she needed to process. She needed to hole herself up somewhere and think about everything that had just happened.

Think about the fact that her mystery pen pal had been in front of her all along.

Her mind flooded with memories of their conversations as the dots connected. It was so obvious now. His mesmerizing green eyes. The way he'd talked about his father, his sister—even losing his mother. His Disney movie knowledge. The dry humor Will had revealed once he'd started to open up to her.

The fact he'd opened up to her at all.

He'd been showing her in little ways he was Closet Poet, and she'd been too blind to see it. Had she stereotyped him that much? Or was she just so stubborn she refused to look under the surface of what she thought she knew?

Or maybe, she thought with a sigh, she was just afraid, plain and simple. Afraid of rejection, of being hurt.

Something he'd been afraid of, too. She couldn't blame him for wanting to minimize that potential, not really. Not when she'd held back, too.

But she could blame him for saying one thing and doing another.

Will—as both himself and Closet Poet—had complained about his father's expectations, but had never done anything to change it. The longer he put it off, the harder it would be, and yet he chose to suffer in silence and resentment.

He said he didn't care what others thought of them as a couple, but could she trust that when he hadn't had the guts to come clean?

But then, who was she to poke at someone's level of courage? Charlotte, Jane, and lately even Will, had been pushing her to leave her situation with Frances ever since she turned eighteen. Longer than that, if she were being honest. And they were right; there was no reason to stay now that she could legally separate herself.

She hadn't wanted to ask herself why she hadn't taken action, despite agreeing with their words. Why she was so adamant she had to wait until graduation.

Was she afraid? Of change, or of Frances? Maybe. When she thought about leaving behind her family home and business, she didn't feel ready. Plus, part of her thought if she stayed working at the café, it was still hers in a way—and she could protect it from the worst of Frances's machinations.

But deep down, another part of her had thought if she could make it through all of high school without letting Frances break her, then she could get through anything. That if she quit before then, she would be giving up on herself.

And if she gave up, she wouldn't deserve a better life.

Which was stupid, of course. It was all a twisted sense of pride. Maybe it made no sense to take pride in being Coffee Girl, the nerdy orphan with an evil stepmother and ridiculous stepsisters, but there it was. She did take pride in it—that it had made her stronger, and, she had to acknowledge, that it made her feel superior.

Wasn't that a kick in the ass.

She had wanted to prove that she could take care of herself; she didn't need help from anyone, didn't need to depend on anyone. She could give herself a better life.

She'd taken support from Charlotte, from Jane, and the others at the café, but hadn't let them help her, not truly. She hadn't wanted to count on them; not when the two people she was supposed to be able to count on most were gone.

That epiphany felt like cool water on a hot day.

At the core of it, she'd only trusted she could count on herself, because history had shown her to count on others was to invite pain and misery.

But that wasn't true. Despite everything, she had proof of that in spades.

She'd never thought of the way Frances treated her as emotional abuse. Neglect maybe, but Will was right. Maybe she should have gone to social services at some point, once she was old enough to understand her situation, but, well, there was that pride again.

What would have been the point? She might have been separated from Jane and Charlotte, from the café and her home, for good. She knew she would leave both eventually, sooner rather than later, but at least she'd had these last years with them.

She pushed back tears as the house came into view. She must

have walked faster than she thought. If Frances and the twins were home, it wouldn't do for them to see her crying.

She went in the front door, went straight for the stairs. Kitty and Lydia must have been waiting for her to come home, because they both came out of the kitchen just as she went up the first few steps.

"Where have you been?" Lydia demanded. "There was no one to make us dinner, and there weren't any leftovers. We had to order takeout!"

"I had to work on a group project for school." Tired, Lizzy just sighed. She wanted to talk to Jane. "You could have made your own dinner."

"As if! Next time, just make sure there's enough leftovers."

"Okay." Lizzy said, then turned and went up the stairs.

"Hey, I wasn't finished!" Lydia called.

"Too bad."

When she got to the top, she sprinted down the hall and up the attic stairs. Making quick work of the locks on her door, she shoved inside, then closed and relocked the door before leaning against it.

Finally, she could breath.

After a few moments, she set her bag on the floor, pulled out her phone, and called Jane.

Pick up. Please pick up, she thought. Just when she thought maybe her friend was with Charlie, she answered.

"Hey, Lizzy." Hearing Jane's bright, cheery voice already went a long way toward calming her. "Is everything okay?"

"Why wouldn't everything be okay?" she hedged, sitting on the edge of her bed.

"Because you're calling me instead of texting."

It was true. She didn't usually call unless it was urgent. "Right.

Well, you'll never believe what just happened. Or maybe you will —you kind of called it."

After a moment of silence, Jane probed. "Well, don't keep me in suspense."

"*Will Darcy* is Closet Poet."

She could not believe she'd just said that out loud. While her brain was processing that, it took a moment for her to realize Jane's response was nowhere near as surprised as she thought it'd be.

"Oh."

"Oh? I just told you my anonymous pen pal, the guy I've been texting for months, the guy I met at the dance, is Will Darcy, and all you can say is 'oh?'"

There was a sheepish shrug in Jane's voice. "Well, I sort of already knew."

"You knew."

"Yeah...Charlie told me."

"Great, so everybody knew but me?"

"No, just me and Charlie. And Will, of course."

"Oh, of course. I feel so much better now."

"Lizzy."

"I'm sorry." She rubbed at her eyes. She knew she couldn't really blame Will for telling Charlie; she'd told Jane after all. And she wouldn't expect Charlie to keep a secret from Jane. "I'm just maybe freaking out a little bit."

"Why? What happened?"

"He almost kissed me."

"Why almost?"

"Because I didn't think it would be fair to Closet Poet, or Will, especially since I kissed Closet Poet at the dance. So I pulled back, and then because it was awkward, he left the room, and I decided to text Closet Poet—and then Will's phone lit up and I saw my name even though I never gave him my number."

"So he didn't tell you?"

"No. I called Closet Poet, and Will's phone rang, which confirmed it. When he came back to the room, we...well, not argued, exactly, but it felt like it. I was upset he'd figured out I'm Lit Fairy and didn't say anything." She explained a little of what had been said. "On the one hand, I don't feel like I can blame him, but on the other, I feel a tiny bit duped."

"That's just your pride talking," Jane told her. "You're embarrassed, so on some level you're blaming him."

"He must think I'm a moron."

"Obviously he doesn't, or he wouldn't have been trying to woo you as himself."

"Woo me? Please."

"Well, what else would you call it?"

Lizzy sighed. "I don't know. But Jane, what am I going to do now? How am I going to face him at school tomorrow?"

"Where's the girl who's courage always rises under intimidation?"

"She's on vacation. She can't make it."

Jane chuckled. "Sure she can."

Sighing again, she lay back on the bed. "I guess I'll find out. Jane?"

"Hm?"

"Thanks for not saying I told you so."

"That part was implied," Jane quipped. "Are you good?"

"Yeah. I'm good. I'll see you tomorrow."

When they'd hung up, Lizzy let her hand flop onto the bed by her side, and she stared up at the ceiling for several minutes.

She wasn't sure how she'd handle tomorrow yet, but Jane was right about one thing. She'd need all the courage she could muster.

As Lizzy hung up with Jane, Kitty and Lydia stepped away from her door, tiptoed quietly back down the attic steps. When they made it to Lydia's room, Lydia whirled on Kitty as though she were responsible.

"I can't believe her! She tricked mom and went to the dance, and this whole time she's had her hooks in Will, texting him. Kissing him!"

Kitty watched as Lydia started to pace, her strides quick and angry. Lydia was an irritable person, easily upset—especially when she was denied something she wanted. "She didn't know it was him," Kitty reminded her, trying to calm her.

"It doesn't matter." Lydia stopped and glared at her sister. "He knew it was her, which is why he didn't want *me*. Somehow that loser made him want *her*. It's all her fault!"

"But—"

Kitty's protest was lost as Lydia practically growled, then threw herself down on the bed. "He was supposed to be mine!"

Kitty pursed her lips but looked away. There was no use disagreeing with Lydia, especially when she was in a snit. She was hoping Lydia would simply forget all about it, but that hope was dashed when Lydia gasped and sat up.

"I got it!" she crowed.

"Got what?"

Lydia's smile was slow and wicked. "Caroline."

"Caroline?"

"Everyone thought she and Will would finally be a thing, but they're not. You heard Lizzy—she's been texting him for months. We could tell Caroline she's trying to steal Will from her."

"But that's not true." Kitty had no idea where Lydia was going with this, but so far she didn't like the sound of it. "Why would we tell her that?"

"Because Caroline has the power to ruin Lizzy." Lydia said it like it was obvious. "She'll be the laughingstock of the school, and Will won't want her anymore."

"Okay..."

When Kitty still didn't seem to be following, Lydia groaned and rolled her eyes, pushing up from the bed with a new resolve.

"Okay. Here's what we're going to do."

Sixteen

LIZZY DIDN'T KNOW what she expected, but for some reason normalcy hadn't been on her list of things to experience on Friday.

Public ridicule had been at the top.

But so far, the school day was progressing as it usually would, with the exception of all the excitement surrounding the championship game. Despite that, she was on edge, like any moment a piano would drop on her head.

Maybe it was because she hadn't seen Will yet.

He'd been coming to her locker in the morning sometimes the past couple weeks; she could assume this was just one of those days when he didn't, but she couldn't help thinking he was avoiding her.

He was very likely as embarrassed as she, and maybe worried she'd still be upset with him. She could—probably should—text him to tell him she wasn't, but she wanted to tell him in person.

What if he just didn't want to see her at all? What if he'd changed his mind and realized she wasn't worth it after all? What if he was mad at her for butting in to his relationship with his dad? The ache in her heart at the thought of those things hinted at the strength of her feelings for him, and she cursed herself for her blindness.

Ah, angst. The basic suffering that pervaded all of human existence, teen or not.

She wouldn't know where she and Will stood until she saw him. Which she would any moment, since the bell for lunch had just rung.

She and Jane were the first at their table, and she waited anxiously for Will, her leg jiggling under the table.

Jane gave her a sympathetic look, held out a bag of Flaming Hot Cheetos. "He'll be here."

"What if it's awkward?"

"Of course it'll be awkward. But then you'll move past it."

Lizzy blew out a breath, grabbed a handful of the spicy treat. "Simple as that, huh?"

Jane opened her mouth to answer, but stopped and smiled; Lizzy followed the direction of her gaze to see Charlie and Will entering the courtyard. Charlie, of course, was beaming, but Will looked...grave. And...nervous? His expression was as inscrutable as ever.

"Stop that." Jane nudged her when she wiggled in her seat.

She froze, but only because Will's gaze snagged on hers. He was still too far away for her to be able to see his eyes, but she felt the intensity of them nonetheless. He kept his eyes on her as he walked, like some invisible tether pulled him—but the tether snapped when a hand came down on his shoulder.

He stopped and turned as Lizzy's eyes scanned the person who'd intercepted him. Her body tensed in confusion when she saw it was Mrs. Matlock, the school principal. Will seemed tense, too, though Mrs. Matlock seemed to be reassuring him of something as she gestured for him to come with her.

Charlie had paused to watch the interaction when Will

stopped, and now Will turned to say something to him before following Mrs. Matlock back inside. Charlie continued to the table alone.

Flicking a worried glance at Lizzy, Jane didn't even wait until Charlie had taken a seat to ask, "What was that about?"

"I guess Will's dad called the school to see if Will could pick up his sister. She got sick at school, but his dad is tied up at the office, and their housekeeper is at a doctor's appointment."

"Is Gianna okay?" Lizzy asked, genuinely worried for her.

"I don't know, but I assume she's with the school nurse," Charlie said. "And Will will take good care of her."

Yes, he would, Lizzy thought. Sure, he doted on his sister, but he was also just good that way. He was probably very worried about Gianna right now, which made her feel guilty for resenting the inconvenient timing. Who knew when she'd get a chance to talk to him now?

She reconsidered waiting to speak to him in person and sending him a message, and even took out her phone. But now definitely was not the time—his focus would be on his sister, as it should be.

She did, however, realize that he was still "Closet Poet" in her phone, and took the opportunity to change it to "Will."

She tried to keep up with conversation for the rest of lunch, but her heart just wasn't in it. She was well and truly moping, and over a guy, no less. Rather than recede, her sense of urgency had only heightened, and she had to work to tamp down the impatience.

If Jane knew what she was thinking, she would tell her it was all going to work out. She could acknowledge it was likely true, but she was having a hard time believing it at the moment.

And she was so ensconced in her thoughts, she never noticed Caroline and Louisa weren't at their table.

Though she disdained the greasy, crumb-covered, wrapper-littered cafeteria, Caroline made an exception for the promise of dirt on Eliza Bennet. She and Louisa grimaced as they sat on the uncomfortable plastic benches of a round table on the far side of the room, adjusted their cheer skirts.

Across from them, the Gardiner twins sat with their (admittedly high end) lunch bags. The blonde one looked nervous, and rightly so—Caroline did not suffer fools—but she despised the way the girl constantly bit at her lip and picked at her fingernails.

The brunette one didn't appear nervous at all. In fact, she seemed downright smug. Caroline could admire that kind of confidence, but she wasn't sure yet that this clandestine meeting was worth her time.

"Thank you for coming." The brunette smiled and folded her hands on the table, all business.

"You said you had information about Elizabeth Bennet. Tell me so I can get out of this dump," Caroline demanded.

The girl sniffed, as if she had any right to be offended. "Fine. We thought you should know Lizzy has been secretly texting Will Darcy for several months, under a different name."

Louisa gasped, but Caroline's eyes narrowed. "That's impossible. Where did you get this information?"

"From the horse's mouth," she said, looking smug again. "Lizzy is our stepsister, and we overheard her talking with her nerdy friend about her plan to capture Will."

"Lydia, are you sure about this?" the nervous one murmured.

"Of course," Lydia snapped. "Someone needs to remind her of her place, and who better than Caroline?"

Now that was more like it.

"I couldn't agree more." For the first time since she'd sat down, a slow smile crept over Caroline's face. "Tell me everything."

Lydia's smile was just as devious. "She used a fake name to reach out to him on social media, and make him fall in love with her. We heard her gloating about how she convinced him to meet her at the dance, and even got him to kiss her."

Caroline grit her teeth. "That little slut. She catfished him?"

Lydia shrugged. "I guess. But like, he knows it was her at the dance. He just doesn't know she planned it."

Of course. It all made sense now.

"That's why he didn't ask me to the dance. Why he's been spending so much time with *her*." Caroline's hands fisted as she pieced it all together. "We'd be together by now if it wasn't for her. How could she do this? She's just a scruffy little...*nobody*."

Lydia shrugged again, as if she could care less. "She's smart. She probably knew just what to say to attract him."

"Well if she thinks she can get away with it, she's got another thing coming." Not if Caroline had anything to say about it. Now that she finally had what she needed to ruin her, it was, as her little informant had said, time to put Elizabeth Bennet in her place.

Lizzy barely paid attention to her surroundings as she dragged her feet to her locker. AP Lit had come and gone, and Will hadn't made an appearance.

Logically, she hadn't expected him to; she'd known he'd stay home with Gianna. But a part of her had still hoped he'd come back for the last class, just to see her. She'd take it as a sign he wasn't mad at her, or was willing to forgive her.

Or at the very least, talk to her.

She was able to convince herself it was wishful thinking; he had no good reason to come back to school when he'd been cleared for the day. But she couldn't convince herself he wasn't avoiding her, for the simple reason that she still hadn't heard from him.

Not a single message since their argument.

It was possible that, like her, he wanted to wait to speak to her in person. Or maybe he was giving her space because he thought she didn't want to talk to him. Or maybe he was embarrassed. Again, logically, she knew they couldn't completely avoid each other forever, and would likely talk it out at some point—it just wouldn't be today.

But part of her—the part with a battered, slightly used self-esteem—thought maybe she'd missed her chance.

That thought had her mood dipping even lower.

She sighed, an undeniably forlorn sound, hoping no one heard as she opened her locker. She pulled out her AP Bio textbook, opening the flap of her messenger bag.

And someone screeched *"Eliza Bennet!"* down the hall, making her jolt.

The book slipped from her fingers, nearly landed on her foot, but she managed to move it just in time. Sighing, she bent to pick up the textbook.

"You!"

Lizzy looked up to see Caroline marching toward her, hands fisted at her sides and her face twisted with absolute malice.

Super, Lizzy thought. *Just what I wanted to brighten my day.* She affected a bored expression as she rose. "How can I help you, Caroline?"

Caroline lifted her chin, folding her arms as she cocked her hip. "You can stay away from my boyfriend."

"You have a boyfriend?" Lizzy arched a brow. "This is the first I'm hearing of it."

"Don't be stupid. You know I'm talking about Will."

"That's funny. I distinctly recall him telling you he'd never be your boyfriend."

"He didn't mean that. It's just the natural way of things—the star quarterback and the head cheerleader. He knows that as well as I do." Caroline sounded confident, but it was all bluster, Lizzy knew. Or delusion.

Lizzy's lips twitched as she slid the book into her bag. "Did he tell you that? Well, then, I guess you don't have to worry about me."

"Don't play dumb. He would be with me already if it weren't for you." She set her hands on her hips, leaned forward as if that would somehow make her more intimidating. "Your weirdo stepsisters told me everything. How you planned to steal him from me —messaging him anonymously, causing him to forget himself. Seducing him at the dance. Can you deny it?"

With a bewildered scoff, Lizzy shut her locker. "Of course I can deny it. I literally just found out Will was the guy I've been messaging *yesterday*."

"You expect me to believe that?" Caroline let out a disbelieving laugh. "You've been cozying up to him ever since the dance."

She took a step forward, gave Lizzy superior once over that said she'd been found wanting.

"You think he'd actually go for someone like you? You're nobody. Just a pathetic, nerdy little coffee girl with nothing to offer."

Lizzy hadn't necessarily been expecting the jibe, but she wasn't surprised. Such a snide and blatantly hurtful comment said far more about Caroline than it did about her.

Whether Will still wanted her or not, she knew with absolute certainty he'd never want someone like Caroline.

"You might have some basic facts, but you don't know me, Caroline." She almost pitied her for holding so tightly to concepts and perceptions that weren't real. "And despite what you think, you don't really know Will, either. This conversation is pointless."

Caroline folded her arms again. "Well, I just wanted to make myself clear."

"Oh, you've made yourself clear," Lizzy assured her. "I've told you there was no convoluted scheme to get Will to notice me, so I'm not sure what else you want from me."

"I want you to give me a straight answer," Caroline bit out. "Are you and Will together?"

If it would make her go away, she might as well give her the truth.

"No, we're not."

Caroline relaxed, her lips curving in satisfaction. "Good. Now promise me you won't date him."

A laugh sputtered up from her throat, and she gave Caroline a look that expressed just how ridiculous that demand was. "Absolutely not. Now if you're done insulting me, I have to get to work."

She turned to leave, but Caroline wasn't finished.

"So you don't care if you ruin him then? That you'll be the laughingstock of the school?"

Pausing, Lizzy sighed as she turned back to face Caroline, gave her a disbelieving look. "No one with any sense would actually care, because it's none of their business. Nor is it yours. I'm sorry to burst your bubble, Caroline, but you're not the boss of me, or Will. Whatever Will and I do is between us, and I will make whatever decision I think will make me happy, without input from you or anyone else whose opinion means nothing to me."

Seething, Caroline glared at Lizzy as though she wanted to incinerate her with her eyes.

"We'll just see what Will has to say about that. You'll wish you'd never crossed me, Coffee Girl."

"Whatever." Ignoring her, Lizzy turned and walked away.

Well, she thought. That was certainly eventful.

And she'd experienced public ridicule after all.

From their vantage point down the hall, Kitty and Lydia observed Caroline's conversation with Lizzy, along with dozens of other students who'd stopped to watch.

Kitty, who knew the outcome wouldn't satisfy Lydia's thirst for revenge, felt uneasy. Watching Caroline stomp down the hall, she said, "She doesn't look happy."

"No, duh." Lydia took off in the opposite direction, toward the parking lot. "We have to do something about this."

"About what?" Kitty asked.

"Lizzy!" Lydia said, like it was obvious. "She thinks she can have Will. He could have been with me, but she distracted him."

"But he said—"

"Well, I won't let her get away with it!" Pulling out her keys, Lydia stalked toward her car. "If Caroline couldn't bring her down, then there's only one person who can."

Seventeen

As AMUSED as she'd been in the face of Caroline's ridiculous and unreasonable demands, in the aftermath, Lizzy's mood had dampened a little. She didn't think much of Caroline Bingley, and definitely didn't care what Caroline thought of her, but it was still hard to be told she was basically worthless.

And in front of the whole school, no less.

Well, not the whole school. But there were a good number of people still in the hallway, and the story would no doubt be all over school by Monday—or maybe even by the game tonight. She tried to remind herself of all the things Will had told her about being the subject of gossip; plus, there was the fact she hadn't let Caroline get to her.

Quack, she thought, and couldn't help smiling a little. That stupid metaphor.

She couldn't say for sure if she'd come out of that confrontation on top, but she hadn't let Caroline beat her down, either—and she hadn't sunk to Caroline's level by insulting her back. She liked to think she'd kept her Cinderella cool.

Despite herself, she kept playing the confrontation over in her mind, analyzing it and wondering if she should have done or said something differently. It was making her antsy. The café wasn't busy, so to keep her hands busy, she grabbed up a rag, started wiping down empty tables.

The routine calmed her a bit, but hadn't really taken her mind off anything. And any peace she might have had went out the window when the bell over the door jangled, and Kitty burst in yelling, "Lizzy!"

"What?" Lizzy snapped, barely sparing her stepsister a glance. She didn't really want to talk to her, knowing she and Lydia must have eavesdropped on her, and gone crying to Caroline. But when Kitty rushed over to her, she was forced to take a second glance, and acknowledge her; and in Kitty's widened eyes, behind her usual nervousness, was genuine fear.

"Lizzy, I'm so sorry—"

"Not now, Kitty." She brushed her off. "I can't talk about the Caroline thing right now, so—"

"No." Kitty interrupted her—and Kitty never interrupted anyone—and gripped her shoulders. "Not that. I mean, I am sorry about that, but...Lydia thought Caroline would humiliate you, and she was so mad when she didn't. I tried to stop her, really."

Dread sank like a stone to the bottom of her stomach, coated her skin with gooseflesh. "What did she do?"

Kitty's expression was more remorseful than she'd ever seen it. "She told Mom you were at the dance. Mom and Lydia went to the bank to drain your accounts; but if you head there now, you can make it in time to stop her. I can drive you."

So it was finally happening. Instinctively, Lizzy knew that things with Frances would soon come to a head—it was time to make it clear she no longer had any power over her. The acknowledgement of that, and the relief of releasing the burden, had her shoulders loosening.

Her face softened enough to give Kitty a small, wry smile. "Thank you, but there's no need. I had her removed from my accounts weeks ago, which I'm sure she'll find out very soon."

"You did?" Kitty relaxed enough to release her shoulders. "Oh. That was smart."

Lizzy nodded. "I had Charlotte take me to the bank the day after I turned eighteen."

At the reminder that Lizzy had semi-recently celebrated a birthday—without any hint from her stepfamily they even knew—Kitty looked sad again. But before she could say anything, the café door slammed open with an ear-shattering *CLANG*, rapping hard into the wall, leaving a dent, and sending the brass bell clattering to the floor.

In unison, Lizzy and Kitty jumped, and whirled to face a livid Frances, Lydia standing behind her with a prim and smug smile. Charlotte, Mary, and Ed all rushed out of the back to join Maddie, who stood frozen at the counter.

"You ungrateful, deceitful little *brat!*" Frances spat. "After everything I've done for you—taking you in, giving you a job—you not only go and deliberately disobey me, you go behind my back. I was just denied access to the account I'm supposed to be a joint owner of. And you know why that is?"

Eyes blazing, Frances took slow, menacing steps toward Lizzy, like a lion stalking its prey. Or perhaps leopard was more accurate, Lizzy mused, as she wore a form fitting, long-sleeved leopard print dress with mile-high hot pink heels. Kitty cringed away, cowering behind Lizzy, but Frances didn't notice her. Lizzy straightened her spine, lifted her chin, and stared Frances down.

"Apparently I was *removed* as an account holder—on my account!" Frances continued. "Well, you won't get away with it, you little thief. I'm putting you under house arrest, but I'm willing to play nice; if you come with me to the bank and put me back as an account owner, I won't have you charged with theft."

Frances stopped a few feet away, waiting expectantly. Charlotte looked like she was about to step in, and the others were just shocked, as were the few patrons sitting at tables.

Lizzy thought she'd be angry, maybe a little afraid. Maybe even a little sad. But now that the moment had come, there was nothing. She felt almost numb, except for the tiny glimmer of long-buried hope in her heart that was starting to claw its way out.

She took a quiet breath, met France's gaze. "Not gonna happen."

"What did you say to me?" Immediately, Frances whipped her phone out of her furry little purse. "I can call the police right now."

"Go right ahead," Lizzy said. "Since the account I removed you from is *mine*, and you were only added in a guardian capacity, you have no legal recourse, or any legal right to my money whatsoever."

"As your guardian, your money is my money." Frances narrowed her eyes. "I have every right."

Now Lizzy smiled a little. "But you're not my guardian anymore. Not for the past several weeks now."

"You don't know what you're talking about."

"I turned eighteen a month ago," Lizzy clarified. "And since I don't trust you, I immediately took steps to ensure you couldn't take any more of what's mine."

Frances stiffened, her eyes going cold. "And this is the thanks I get for everything I've done for you, you—"

"And what exactly have you done for me?" Lizzy asked, more calmly than she felt. "Banishing me to the attic? Turning me into your unpaid housekeeper? Alternately ignoring me and degrading me? Well, I'm done with all of it—done with you."

Heart pounding now, she very intentionally dropped the rag

she held on the floor. "I quit. And no need to whine about keeping a roof over my head anymore—I intend to move out as soon as possible."

Frances had stood blinking and slack-jawed, but now her lips upturned in an amused sort of skepticism. "And just where do you think you'll live? And without a job to pay rent?"

"That's easy." Deciding it was the perfect time to enter the conversation, Charlotte stepped around the counter to go stand beside Lizzy. "Lizzy knows she always has a place with me."

Then, flashing Frances a wicked smile, she said, "Oh, and by the way, I quit, too."

Beaming, Lizzy offered her arm to Charlotte. "Whaddaya say we blow this popsicle stand?"

Looping her arm through Lizzy's, Charlotte beamed back. "Don't mind if I do."

Arm in arm, they brushed past Frances and Lydia, whose expressions had turned sour, to take off their aprons and get their belongings from the back.

"You'll regret this," Frances shouted after them. "You need me!"

Lizzy hefted her bag onto her shoulder as she and Charlotte came back out, gave Frances a quizzical look. "What I regret is not doing this sooner. You don't care two figs about me, Frances. I doubt you'll even notice I'm gone."

And with that, the two women sailed out of the café where they'd both worked for many years with nary a backward glance.

For Lizzy it was bittersweet—she was finally free of Frances, or nearly so, but she had to leave behind the family business that had always been part of her life.

But Bookish Brews had been gone for a while. It was time to let go.

"I'm guessing," Charlotte said as they approached her car down the block, "You want to go pack some things now."

"That would be great," Lizzy admitted. "I want to pack as much as possible; I don't trust Frances not to call a locksmith and toss my stuff just to spite me."

"Then that's what we'll do."

"Can I help?" asked a timid voice.

They turned to see Kitty had followed, and she wrung her hands when they stopped to look at her. Behind her, outside the door of the café, Frances and Lydia were glaring in their direction.

"Are you sure you want to do that?" Lizzy asked.

As if she could feel the eyes on her, Kitty stiffened her spine a little, and for once, she didn't quibble. "Yes."

"Alright, then," Charlotte said softly.

"We've got a little time," Kitty added. "Mom said she's going to see what her lawyer has to say about all this. That might take a while."

Lizzy exchanged a look with Charlotte. "Then we better use it wisely."

So far, the day had not gone as planned, Will thought wearily. He'd meant to talk to Lizzy at lunch, but Gianna's emergency had derailed everything. Gianna was fine now, and she was in good hands with Mrs. R., but it was still hard to see her sick.

And now, as much as he wanted to head to the café to see Lizzy, everyone would flip out if he didn't show up for the game.

As he headed out to his car to leave, Caroline's little red sports car zipped up to the curb outside his house. He heard her door slam as he tossed his gear bag into the trunk.

"Will!" As she stormed up the drive, indignation in her eyes, he braced himself for the tantrum he'd been expecting. "You will never believe what that...*nobody*, Elizabeth Bennet, said to me today!"

"You spoke to Elizabeth?"

He couldn't for the life of him think why Lizzy would talk to Caroline, or vice versa, but he could well imagine that Caroline would be unsatisfied with the result.

"Of course—I had to set her straight." She splayed her hands. "Those stepsisters of hers informed me how she pulled you in, tricked you into falling for her. Somebody had to put her in her place. She denied the whole thing, of course, but she's not who you think she is."

He had a bad feeling he knew what kind of nonsense Caroline had spewed at Lizzy. "Set her straight?" he asked warily.

"Yes. I told her she was destined to fail, since you'll come to your senses eventually and ask me out." She punctuated the statement with a coy look and a bat of her lashes before continuing, "I told her to stay away from you, and you know what she said to me?"

He didn't bother asking what since she was clearly geared up to tell him.

"She laughed at me!" Caroline threw her arms up before placing her hands on her hips.

He could imagine it well, and his lips twitched at the thought. "The insolence."

"*And.*" Completely missing his blandly amused tone, she worked herself up to pacing. "When I asked her to promise not to date you, she flat out refused."

His head snapped to her face, eyes locking on hers. "She did?"

"Yes!" Relieved he understood what she was getting at, Caroline huffed, then gave him a commiserating smile. "She's after you, Will, even if it ruins you. She had the gall to say it was none of my business, and she'd do whatever makes her happy, no matter if she'd be a laughingstock. She even thinks no one would care if you were with a loser like her."

She'd stepped closer as she spoke, running a hand down his arm, and rolling her eyes at the last statement. Hope welled up in him, burst like a geyser.

If Lizzy were truly set against him, he knew she would have no problem saying so to Caroline. But she hadn't. She may not have said it directly—especially not to Caroline—but Lizzy had inadvertently indicated she did have feelings for him. Or at the very least, she'd forgiven him, which meant there was still hope.

He didn't realize a wide smile had broken over his face until Caroline pressed into him, and when he looked down at her, she tilted her face up like she expected him to kiss her. Why, after he'd stated clearly he wasn't interested in her, she persisted in thinking otherwise baffled him.

Maybe it was her turn to be set straight.

He grinned openly, looked right into her eyes, and said, "She's right."

Smile melting, Caroline blanched as though someone had tossed a bucket of water over her head. "What?"

"She's right about everything." He held her gaze, his eyes hard despite the smile still on his face. "Most people wouldn't care who I date, and if they do, that's their problem. And she didn't trick me into anything. She hasn't been after me; if anything, I've been after her—and let me tell you, it hasn't been easy gaining her good opinion."

Shaking her head as though it would erase what she was hearing, Caroline whined, "You can't mean that."

"Oh, but I do. You had no right to say those things to her, to stick your nose in my business. But I can't tell you how glad I am you did, because you've just told me I still have a chance with her."

Caroline narrowed her eyes. "You can't actually be choosing *her* over *me*."

"I'm not choosing her over anyone. I'm just choosing her."

Moving around her, he walked around the car to the driver's side, indicating the conversation was over.

"Will!"

Caroline still looked like she couldn't believe what was happening, watching him with her mouth agape like a fish.

"Oh, and in case it was unclear—there is no situation in which I would choose you." Ignoring how her jaw dropped even further, he opened the door, climbed into the driver's seat. "Now, if you don't mind, I've got to get to the game—and so do you."

She finally shut her mouth, blinking rapidly. As he shut the door, her mouth twisted, and she stomped her foot, letting out a primal, toddler-approved scream.

He started the car, inched by her. As he pulled away, he could see her storming back to her car in his rearview mirror.

Hopefully that would be the end of it.

As he drove to the high school, his good mood deflated a little when he realized he'd have to wait to talk to Elizabeth. She was probably working tonight, so he wouldn't see her at the game, and afterword it might be too late, so he likely wouldn't get to talk to her until tomorrow.

He'd have to hold on to his hope until then.

Eighteen

CHARLOTTE PARKED across the street from the house, and Kitty pulled into the driveway. While Kitty rummaged through the garage for some boxes, Lizzy led Charlotte up to her room.

"I haven't been inside this house in years," Charlotte remarked, running a hand along a wall where family photos used to hang. There was no need for her to mention why. "So much has changed."

Looking away from where Charlotte's fingers grazed the wall —now covered in peacock patterned wallpaper and professional modeling shots of Frances—Lizzy continued down the hall, toward the attic stairs.

"Well, you know Frances. She has to leave her mark on everything."

When she unlocked the door to her room, she immediately pulled her suitcase and a duffel bag from under her bed, tossed them on top of it. As she opened the suitcase, her eyes caught on the hamper in the corner of the room. It wasn't empty, but there wasn't much in it since she did the laundry frequently; and since they lacked packing vessels, she figured it would be the perfect thing to transport her clothes in.

She gestured to the rack of her hanging clothes. "Can you see how much of that will fit in the hamper?"

When Charlotte nodded, got to work, Lizzy went to her dresser, started pulling out clothes and putting them in the suitcase, then when that was full, the duffel. It was a small dresser, and a small rack, but clothes took up more space than she thought. They'd just managed to fit all her clothes in the bags and the hamper when Kitty finally made it upstairs, lugging several broken down cardboard boxes.

Breathing heavily, she let them fall to the floor. "I had...to break them...down first."

"Thank you, Kitty." Lizzy didn't ask what had been in the boxes, or what Kitty had done with the contents. As the three of them refolded the boxes, Lizzy considered what most needed to be packed.

Without being asked, Kitty went to the bookshelf and began carefully fitting as many books as she could inside. Grateful, Lizzy set a box on top of her desk, and started going through her drawers. In the left drawer was a box of family photos and trinkets, and she placed that in there first. Turning to the dresser, she picked up her jewelry box, put that in next. Then she emptied out the rest of the desk drawers—an assortment of notebooks, pens and pencils, and office supplies. From her nightstand, she grabbed her phone charger, her flashlight, and the Swiss Army knife her dad had given her for her tenth birthday.

When she'd finished, she saw Kitty had filled her box with books and was starting on another. Charlotte had pulled out her fireproof safe from under the bed—that could be carried on its own—tossed what few pairs of shoes she owned in one of the smaller boxes, and had neatly folded up her bedding into another box. She was now in the little half-bath packing up Lizzy's toiletries.

Since that was—sadly—nearly everything, Lizzy went to her bedside lamp, unplugged it. Kitty paused in confusion to watch her as she turned it over, began to unscrew the bottom.

"Whoa," Kitty whispered when Lizzy dumped out the cash she had stashed inside. "That is so cool."

Standing to examine the lamp, Kitty's eyes widened. "Can you tell me where you got this? Lydia likes to take my stuff sometimes."

Considering, Lizzy screwed the bottom back on, then held out the lamp. "Here. Why don't you just take this one?"

Kitty blinked, cautiously taking the lamp as though the gesture were a trick. "You don't want it?"

Lizzy shrugged. "I don't need it anymore. And Lydia will be less suspicious of something new in your room if it came from mine."

Kitty's eyes welled, and to Lizzy's surprise, she threw her arms around her. "Thank you, Lizzy. I don't deserve you being so nice to me."

"Think of it as a thank you for helping me gift." As Lizzy lightly hugged Kitty back, she could see Charlotte watching them with a soft expression, and it reminded her of something her dad had said once. When she pulled back, she gave Kitty a supportive smile. "Everyone deserves kindness."

Kitty sniffled, her lips curving slightly. "Even my mom?"

"Yes," Lizzy said, though reluctantly. "I did her the kindness of not telling her what I really think of her, satisfying as that would be."

A small laugh bubbled out of Kitty.

"Maybe it's small of me, but I have no such compunction," Charlotte said, stepping out of the bathroom. "The only reason I didn't tell that woman off was because we were in public."

"I'd pay to see that," Lizzy quipped, putting her cash stash in her messenger bag.

They made quick work of the rest of the books, which took up three boxes in total, and quickly loaded almost everything into Charlotte's car. They'd just gone back upstairs for the last few boxes when they heard Frances and Lydia get home.

"Why is the front door open?" Frances shrieked.

Bracing themselves, they carried the boxes down the stairs, and at the bottom, Frances waited, hands on her hips and eyes flaring. Her lack of smug disdain told Lizzy the lawyer hadn't told Frances what she wanted to hear.

"What do you think you're doing?"

"I told you," Lizzy said blandly. "I'm moving out."

Frances sniffed, eyed the boxes. "I'm not letting you leave without looking through those boxes. I want to make sure you didn't take anything that doesn't belong to you."

Lizzy let her disgust show as she ran her eyes over her stepmother's tacky outfit. "I can assure you wholeheartedly I don't want anything of yours. And there's no way I'm letting you paw through my things."

When her mouth twisted, Lizzy was sure Frances was about to unleash the full force of her fury—but Kitty stepped out from behind Charlotte, gripped the box she held a little tighter.

"She didn't take anything that wasn't hers." Her voice was a little shaky at first, but she swallowed and forced her voice to come out a little stronger. "I made sure of it."

"Traitor," Lydia spat. "Why are you helping her?"

Kitty blinked, then shrugged. "You wanted her gone, didn't you? It's faster this way."

Lizzy fought to keep her lips from twitching. Kitty was definitely smarter than she seemed; her responses seemed to mollify both mother and daughter, so Lizzy stepped the rest of the way down the stairs. She pushed past Frances, whose eyes tracked her—though, thankfully, she said nothing more. Lydia stuck out her tongue as she passed by.

Just as she reached the threshold of the front door, Frances spoke. "You better not come back here. You step one foot on my property, and I'll have you arrested for trespassing."

Lizzy paused in the doorway. Without turning around she said, "Goodbye, Frances. Thanks for nothing."

She'd walked down the steps, Kitty close behind her, when she heard Charlotte's voice.

"You know Frances, I've always thought you were a small, spineless, petty, vicious woman. And today, you've proven me right."

With that, Charlotte exited the house, joining Lizzy and Kitty as they walked to her car. Lizzy murmured a silent goodbye to the gnomes as she passed them.

I'll miss you the most, Undertaker, she thought.

Frances watched eagle-eyed from the doorway as they loaded the boxes, and Lizzy finally let herself wonder what would happen to Kitty now that she'd defied her mother—and her twin.

"You going to be alright?" she asked her.

Kitty nodded. "They both might be annoyed with me for a little bit, but mom always focuses on Lydia, and it won't take Lydia long to go back to thinking of me as her sidekick."

Lizzy barely refrained from wincing—she'd often thought of Kitty as nothing more than Lydia's sidekick. It wasn't hard to understand why Kitty felt that way, too.

"Catherine," Charlotte said in her protective, nurturing way, and Kitty's eyes widened hearing her given name. "If Frances makes things hard for you, you let me know."

"Okay." She turned to Lizzy. "I'd give you a hug, but..."

"I know. I'll see you at school."

Kitty pursed her lips for a moment, then said. "You should go to the game."

"The game?"

"Yeah. When was the last time you went to one? Besides," Kitty smiled. "You can support Will. There's a lot of pressure on him tonight."

"Yeah. Maybe."

With one last nod, Kitty went back inside. Lizzy climbed into the passenger seat of Charlotte's car, looked back at the house as she buckled in. Then she faced forward, determined not to look back as Charlotte drove them away.

She considered Kitty's words on the way, mulled them over as they carried her stuff into the little guest room of Charlotte's house.

"Do you want to unpack now?" Charlotte asked her.

"No," Lizzy said as she determined what to do. "Kitty's right. I should go to the game. And if I could talk to Will..."

Charlotte smiled. "Alright then. I won't wait up."

Lizzy checked her watch. The game didn't start for a half hour, which meant she just had enough time to change. She pulled out her phone, sent Jane a quick text.

> Hey! Long story short, I quit my job, and moved in with Charlotte. Think you can pick me up for the game tonight?

She chuckled a little when the response came.

JANE

> What?!!! 😼 😺 FINALLY. That's awesome! And of course I'll pick you up.

> Thank you. I owe you all the Flaming Hot Cheetos.

Yes, you do. Also, I need the full story ASAP.

Don't worry, you'll get it.

Feeling freer and more optimistic than she had in a while, Lizzy set her phone aside, and prepared to go cheer on the guy she liked at the championship football game.

For the first time ever, she was a cliché—and she didn't mind it at all.

Nineteen

"*Oof.*"

For what felt like the hundredth time, Will hit the turf, this time hard enough to rattle some bones. The body that had slammed into him grunted, rising as other players surrounded them. Will gave himself a moment before sitting up himself, letting the ball in his arms slide to the ground.

Charlie's helmeted face came into view, and he held out a hand. Will gripped it, let his friend help him to his feet.

"That one looked like a doozy," Charlie said.

"Yep," Will groaned.

"You okay? You seem..."

"Out of it? Unfocused? You can say it." He turned to jog back to where Coach was waving them over. Since that last play had lost them the offense, they'd get to sit down for a bit. "My head's not in the game."

He was distracted, and he knew it—and he knew he'd hear about it.

"It's on Lizzy." Charlie said knowingly.

"Yeah."

Coach eyed him as he and Charlie took a bench, pulled off their helmets, grabbed up water bottles. As he squeezed a stream of water into his mouth, Charlie said, "I would've thought having her here would cheer you up."

"What? She's here?" He couldn't recall Lizzy attending a football game once.

Charlie turned and pointed into the stands. "Yeah, she's sitting with Jane."

Will shifted and followed the direction of Charlie's gaze. His breath caught when he spotted Lizzy, head bent in conversation with Jane, fiddling with the sleeve of the black zip-up hoodie she wore over a red t-shirt in an effort to wear their team colors.

Did he dare hope she'd come for him?

A movement caught his eye, drew his attention to the fence bordering the track. His father was waving to him, and when he finally looked over, his dad narrowed his eyes, tapped his temple, and Will knew he was telling him to get his head on straight. Then he turned and headed back to the stands.

Sighing, Will turned and gave his attention to his team. The fact Lizzy had come to the game was a good sign; he just had to get through the game, and then he could focus on her.

His team was counting on him.

When, at the end of the first half, their opponent was up nine to zero, he knew his work was cut out for him. He looked up into the bleachers where Elizabeth and Jane still sat as the team made their way to the locker room for their halftime break, hoping to catch Lizzy's eye, but she was looking out at the field.

In the locker room, they did a review of their first half, and Coach went over some plays he wanted to consider for the second.

He listened with half an ear as Coach grilled him for his

distraction in the first half, then did his duty and gave the expected pep talk to his team, though his heart wasn't really in it. He suspected Charlie was the only one who could tell though, and, good friend that he was, took up the mantle of properly hyping up their team.

All too soon their break was over, and it was time to get back to the game.

Wanting to put it off, he slowed his jog, falling back and trailing behind the rest of the team as they headed back onto the field to the cheers and wolf-howling of the crowd.

Of course his mind immediately drifted to Elizabeth. He thought he'd screwed his chances with her, but Caroline's rant had given him hope. And once he'd noticed Elizabeth sitting with Jane, watching the game, even deigning to cheer for the team, that hope had doubled.

How was he going to make it through the second half when all he wanted was to talk to her? Impatient as he was, he didn't want to let his team down.

"Will."

A voice stopped him when he passed by the side of the bleachers. He turned his head to see Kitty Gardiner, shuffling her feet from side to side.

She bit her lip. "Can I talk to you?"

He narrowed his eyes, sent her a stony expression. "I know you and Lydia said something to Caroline about Lizzy. I don't want to hear anything you have to say."

Even as he turned, she stepped forward. She stopped when she saw he kept walking, and he thought that would be the end of it, but she called out to him.

"Lizzy quit the café."

He halted in his tracks, whipped around. Several thoughts

rushed through his brain, but at the forefront was, "What? What happened?"

Kitty stopped fidgeting, and it surprised him when her expression turned remorseful.

"Lydia was mad after Lizzy told Caroline to shove it. She thought Caroline would hurt Lizzy, but Lizzy only made Caroline angry. So she decided to tell our mom Lizzy had gone to the dance. I tried to convince her not to, but..."

"Kitty. What. Happened."

"My mom went to the café and started yelling at Lizzy. Saying all these horrible things. I guess that was the last straw for Lizzy, because she told Mom off, quit her job, and said she was moving in with Charlotte."

Pride swelled in him as he imagined it. His brilliant, fiery Lizzy taking on the one thing that had kept her down. "She did?" he said, almost reverently.

Smiling a little now, Kitty nodded. "She did. It was totally epic."

"I bet it was." Then the smile that had formed at the thought slowly turned down as he really looked at Kitty. "Why are you telling me this?"

Kitty glanced at her feet for a moment, then straightened her shoulders and looked back up. "Because I'm sorry. I know I can't change all the years I was mean to Lizzy, or did nothing to stop my mom from mistreating her, but I can at least try to fix something I helped break."

Maybe there was hope for her yet, he thought as he nodded. "That's a good start. Thank you."

She gave him a sad smile. "What are you going to do now?"

What a loaded question. "Something I should have done a while ago."

"Hey, Will, c'mon man."

They both looked over to see Ricky, who'd backtracked to round up the straggler.

"I'm coming," Will assured him.

"Good luck," Kitty said, and something told him she wasn't referring to the game.

Ricky didn't know that though, and, letting his eyes travel over her, he grinned. "Thanks."

Kitty blushed, but smiled.

Internally, Will rolled his eyes. "Okay, Casanova. Woo the lady later."

He nodded to Kitty as he clapped Ricky on the back, and the two of them turned to leave. He sought out Lizzy in the crowd, and finding her still sitting with Jane, *later* sounded incredibly far away.

Now that he was on a mission, Will was nearly giddy with excitement. If Lizzy could stand up to her stepmom, he could stand up to his dad—and for the first time, the idea of doing so brought him relief instead of stress.

He knew what he wanted to do, which was go talk to Lizzy right that moment, but he also knew his team was relying on him. Besides, he wanted to finish out the game.

He was a Darcy after all, and Darcys always finished what they started.

Lizzy could feel nerves zipping around under her skin, but she couldn't explain why. Maybe she was just coming down from the adrenaline rush of the day, but whatever it was, she was still nervous.

Something was off with Will—he wasn't playing as well as he

normally did. At least, she assumed so. She'd picked up on some of the murmurs going around the stands, speculating as to what was going on with him.

Many thought perhaps it was some performance anxiety. It was the big game after all.

A lot of that speculation turned to her, however, and she'd lost count of the times she'd felt eyes on her throughout the first half of the game.

Something told her he *was* thinking about her, just as she was thinking of him. She wondered if Caroline had did as she'd threatened, and gone to tell Will about their encounter. She wondered what he made of it if she did.

Maybe that's what she was nervous about. What if Caroline had twisted her words, or straight up lied? Will might not believe her, or not entirely, but it might still complicate things.

When the team headed back out to the field, her eyes automatically searched for Will, but she didn't see him. She carefully scanned each player, but no, he definitely wasn't there.

Which begged the question: where was he?

She didn't realize how tense she was until she finally spotted him rushing onto the field a minute or so later, her whole body sagging in relief.

And then, to her surprise, he turned to look into the stands—right at her. It was hard to tell exactly what he was looking at with his helmet on, but she was positive he was looking at her. She straightened, and though she didn't dare draw attention to herself by waving, she gave him a small smile.

He tipped his head a little, in what she assumed was a surreptitious nod. She was so focused on him that she startled a little when the buzzer sounded loud and glaring from the scoreboard, signaling the start of the second half.

Her nervousness made her edgy all over again. She'd never

cared for football, and she didn't really care now—except for the fact that Will was playing. She winced every time someone tackled him, holding her breath until it was clear he was uninjured.

How did anyone sit through this? It was both boring and nerve wracking at the same time.

She knew the basics of the game—how touchdowns and field goals were scored and how many points they were worth, what many of the positions were, and the gist of offense and defense. But the yard lines baffled her—the cheerleaders had done a cheer during the first half with the words 'first and ten,' and while she understood they were referring to the ten yard line, she had no idea what the phrase meant.

She understood a little better when Jane explained to her what a 'down' was, but she still didn't quite grasp it.

She was on her feet with the rest of the crowd, however, when the Wolves conducted a play that enabled Will to slink past the other team long enough to make a break for the end zone. A couple players from the opposing team were hot on his heels, but he was fast enough to dodge and outrun them.

"Woo!" She cupped her hands over her mouth to howl like a wolf with everyone else, waited in anticipation to see what they'd do next.

There was more cheering when the field goal was successful, and the score was tied; the crowd collectively retook their seats, breathing sighs of relief.

She heard more than one comment saying something like "Will's back."

Maybe she was getting her hopes up, but she liked to think their tacit moment just before the second half had steadied him. That, or just knowing she was here.

He had to know she was here to support him, right?

Maybe it was the craziness of the day, but she just had the

feeling everything would work out the way it should, something she wasn't sure she'd ever truly felt before.

She kept her eyes on Will, and there were a couple times between plays when he looked at the stands that had her wondering if he was seeking her out again. And other than knowing what the score was, she wasn't sure what else was happening in the game.

Before long, there were only a handful of minutes left in the game, and the score was still tied. The clock seemed almost ominous in the way it continued to run down. When Ricky, in a stroke of luck, intercepted the ball from the opposing team, the crowd roared, buzzing with excitement now that victory was within reach.

The Wolves' coach finally called a time out to stop the clock, and all eyes turned, once again, to Will. Especially, Lizzy noted, Robert Darcy.

He'd left the stands, going instead to stand at the fence, arms folded on top as he leaned against it. Beside him was another man, wearing a uniformed jacket and cap that seemed to scream "I'm a coach!" Something told her he was just as interested in Will as Robert.

She swallowed a lump in her throat. Did Will know this guy was here to watch him? Likely he did, but how he felt about it was another story.

She didn't want to jump to conclusions, but at the very least it was clear he hadn't talked to his dad about his real goals.

Anticipation dashed, she returned her attention to the field, where the team huddled together. Already she missed the confidence she'd felt earlier, of knowing things would work out. She tried to remind herself what was meant to be would be. And she wouldn't know what would be until she could talk to Will.

If it had felt like the game was dragging before, it was absolutely sluggish now. She didn't actually care if they won, but she prayed for the Wolves to score if only so they wouldn't go into overtime.

When the team broke their huddle, she scooted to the edge of her seat.

Twenty

IN THE HUDDLE, Will glanced at the faces of his teammates—some anxious, some revved, some expectant. Regardless, he knew they all thought he would lead them to victory, so he intended to do his best.

He explained what would hopefully be their final play.

"Everyone got that?"

They all nodded their assent.

"Charlie, you ready?" he asked his friend.

Another nod. "Let's do this."

They broke and took up their positions, and for the first time in the game, Will's nervousness had nothing to do with Elizabeth, and everything to do with the game at hand. They didn't have much time left, and he could feel the energy pulsing in the air around him—of the players, of the crowd, of his rapidly beating heart.

His team wanted to win, and he was right there with them.

He called out, setting the play in motion, everyone on the field tensing before splitting apart in a flurry. Will held on to the ball and weaved around, evading other players and trusting his team to cover him, before finally finding a break.

His eyes sought out Charlie, who'd nearly made it to the end zone, free and clear. A shout told him he'd been noticed, and likely Charlie had, too; he took off to avoid being tackled as Charlie kept going, but looked back for Will.

Glancing behind him, Will decided he had enough time to make the throw, but he'd have to be quick about it. Charlie raised up his hands, and Will pivoted, rearing his arm back and launching the ball to Charlie.

The ball went spinning, and not a moment too soon, as he was tackled from behind. The ball was in Charlie's hands in seconds, and as another player came up on him, he turned and sprinted the last several yards, leaping out of reach of the tackle and into the end zone.

Charlie slammed the ball to the ground in triumph as the crowd stomped their feet in the bleachers. There was still a minute left on the clock, but they could run it down.

They tried to do so by making a play for the extra point; though they failed to get the extra point, they did draw it out enough for the time to dwindle down to a handful of seconds.

And as the timer buzzed, a roar erupted from the crowd, a cacophony of howls. Even as Will exhaled, the wind was knocked out of him when Ricky practically jumped on him, bouncing on his toes and throwing an arm over Will's shoulders, hooting in victory. More of their teammates joined, until the whole team was cheering and enacting their own victory dances.

When Will finally looked back at the stands, he saw half the crowd had filed out of the bleachers, and were filtering onto the field. Family, friends, and supporters were racing toward their players, excitement and pride lining their faces.

Instinctively, Will looked for Lizzy.

Instead, he saw his dad walking toward him, beaming wider, and certainly more proudly, than he'd seen in a while.

And right behind him was a man in a Stanford coach's uniform.

Looks like it's time, he thought as he pulled off his helmet. It had never been more clear he should have told his dad about his dreams—or lack thereof—earlier, as this moment was bound to cause them both some embarrassment.

Couldn't be helped, he supposed.

"Will! That was incredible." His father gave him a hard slap on the back. "I was a little worried there, considering who was watching—your first half was a little sloppy. But you really came through."

For once, he didn't let the criticism-laced compliment get to him. "Thanks."

"I wanted you to meet Coach Forster, the head of Stanford's football team."

"Hi, Will. I've heard a lot of great things about you." Forster said, holding out his hand. "And I can honestly say none of it was exaggerated. It was a great game."

"It's nice to meet you, sir." Will shook his hand politely, but without any enthusiasm. "And thank you."

Forster smiled, and Will knew what was coming before he said, "I'm sure you've guessed, but we'd love to have you next year."

"I appreciate that, sir." His father looked on, expectant and still smiling. Will paused to take a breath, feeling a little guilty knowing that satisfied look would be wiped away when he continued, "Unfortunately, I can't accept."

As his dad's proud smile instantly turned on itself, Forster's turned to one of confusion. "What do you mean?"

"I like football, but I have no interest in playing beyond high school, or in attending Stanford," Will clarified, making sure to catch his dad's eye. "I'm sorry for the confusion, and for wasting your time."

A movement out of the corner of his eye caught his attention, and he turned his head to see Lizzy approaching, Jane at her side. Jane must have spotted Charlie, because she grinned from ear to ear and ran off, while Lizzy's grin was all for him.

She'd come for *him*.

Even as he smiled back, his dad gripped his shoulders, literally shook him out of his daze. "William Darcy, what do you think you're doing? Your future is at stake here."

"No, Dad, it isn't. It's just a different future than the one you imagined."

He imagined the smile on his face was a little dopey, but he didn't care, and even his dad's anger couldn't remove it.

What did nearly remove it was when he noticed Lizzy had stopped in her tracks. She was no longer smiling, or looking at him —instead she was focused on Forster, her eyes skipping from the coach to his dad before finally settling back on him.

Disappointment was clear on her face. She must have thought he was choosing Stanford after all, because she gave him a sad smile, and turned away. He'd have to continue this conversation later.

Brushing his dad off, he nodded to Forster. "Nice to meet you. Good luck next year."

He stepped away, starting to jog toward Lizzy, but his dad followed; he must have noticed Lizzy, too, because he caught up after several steps and laid a hand on his chest. The mix of shock and upset was still clear on his face when he said, "You're giving up on your future for a girl?"

A slow grin took over Will's face. "I'm not giving up on anything. I'm finally going after what *I* want, instead of what *you* want."

He broke away, and almost as an afterthought, handed him the helmet he'd forgotten was in his hand. And as if to emphasize the moment, the crowd let out another unanimous cheer as their coach held up the championship trophy. He needed to find Lizzy before he got sucked into the congratulations and picture-taking.

Thankfully the density of the crowd kept her from getting too far, and he spotted her only a few feet away.

"Lizzy!" He called after her.

She stopped, hesitated, then turned and waited for him to catch up, arms folded across her chest.

"What are you doing?" she asked when he reached her. He saw her eyes dart to the team, and their celebration.

"Will!" They both turned their heads to look at his dad, who, he noted, seemed caught between wanting to storm over in outrage or standing frozen with shock. Out of the corner of his eye he could also tell the shout had drawn some attention. But this time he ignored the summons and, turning back to Lizzy, gazed into those hopeful, hypnotic eyes.

"Kitty," he said, a little breathless. "She told me you stood up to Frances."

"She did?"

"Yeah. She said it was, and I quote, 'totally epic.'"

A small, incredulous laugh escaped her. "It seems my hope in Kitty was not misplaced."

Shaking his head, he grinned. "And Caroline."

"Oh, God." Now her hand came up, and she pinched the bridge of her nose. "Do I even want to know what happened?"

"She told me you refused not to date me."

Her head immediately whipped up. When she saw the ridiculous grin on his face, a slow smile spread over her own.

"Did she now?" This time the question was sly, flirtation dancing in her eyes.

"I'm sure she thought I would be disgusted by your presumption." He took a chance and placed his hands on her arms, drew her closer, which had the added effect of trapping her arms between them. "But it had the opposite effect—it gave me hope that I hadn't ruined things between us."

"Ruined? If anyone ruined things, it was me." She kept her eyes on her hands, which had settled on his chest, and spread her fingers. Not for the first time, he cursed the stupid, bulky shoulder pads of his uniform. "I freaked out. And you were right about everything."

"It doesn't matter. And you were right, too."

She looked up at him now, eyes glinting with something new. Dare he call it affection—or maybe even love?

"So what do we do now, Prince Charming?"

"Now I kiss you, Cinderella." He lifted a hand to cup her cheek, tilted her face up to meet his. And as their noses brushed, he pulled back a little. "Oh, and we live happily ever after."

She gave him a delighted smirk, sliding her hands up to cup the back of his neck. "Can't forget the happily ever after."

Then she yanked his head down and crushed her lips to his.

She'd remember this moment forever, Lizzy thought. Even more than the kiss they'd shared at the dance—this one was pure fairytale magic.

She rose on her toes as Will's arms came around her waist, reveling in the feel of his lips as they explored hers. A tingle went through her when he switched angles, dipped his tongue into her mouth, and she hummed when it tangled with hers.

He pressed his lips against hers just a little harder, lingering for a moment before lifting his head.

"How's that for happily ever after?"

"Oh, you killed it," she assured him. "Is everyone staring at us?"

He turned his head toward the center of the celebration. "Not...everyone."

The way he said it—half amusement, half grimace—had her eyes darting to the crowd, where she spotted several familiar faces looking at them.

Caroline Bingley stood with Louisa on the track, managing to look absolutely crushed while shooting daggers at them. Farther afield, Lydia wore a similar expression, while Kitty stood behind her, giving a subtle thumbs up.

Standing with the rest of team, Charlie and Jane had paused amid their own celebration to grin heartily at them; beside them, Ricky's expression was equally wide, and Anne waved shyly while hand in hand with a fellow cheerleader—Jenny, Lizzy assumed.

And of course, there was Will's dad.

Not awkward at all, Lizzy thought wryly, even as she saw he was watching them with something like understanding.

Other classmates had glanced in their direction, some smiling, some wide-eyed, and Lizzy found she didn't care. It didn't matter anymore.

Because she had Will. The guy she'd wanted and the guy she hadn't realized she needed, all wrapped up in one perfectly imperfect, undeniably handsome package. The brooding poet, the popular jock, the doting older brother, the Darcy son, the nerd, and the reserved soul—she finally understood he was all of them.

Chuckling, she turned back to him, and he looked at her curiously.

"What's so funny?"

She shook her head. "I'm just laughing at myself for not realizing how charming you are sooner."

Now he chuckled. "Boy, did I have my work cut out for me. Who knew wooing a princess would be so hard?"

"Maybe that's because I'm no princess, and therefore am not impressed by your princely ways."

"What was that you were saying, about realizing how charming I am?"

"It wasn't the prince that charmed me," she reminded him. "It was the guy behind the mask."

He drew her closer, leaned his forehead against hers. "If not for you, I might still be wearing it."

She rose on her toes to give him a long, heartfelt kiss before asking, "So what now? Do you want to join your team in celebrating?"

"Nah, they don't need me for that." He grinned, a little wickedly. "Wanna get out of here?"

Did she ever.

"Absolutely."

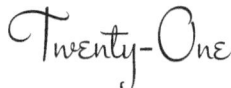

Twenty-One

Seven Months Later

WITH WILL'S arm slung over her shoulder, holding her close, Lizzy leaned against him, tipping her head against his chest as they watched the scene in front of them.

The café was closed to the public for the day, and all their friends and family had gathered together to celebrate the culmination of their high school careers. As she had many times over the past several months, Lizzy mused how vastly different it looked, restored to its former glory—including the sign above the awning once more reading *Bookish Brews* instead of *Frances's*.

It was one of the many ways life had changed since that fateful Friday in October. It almost felt like a whirlwind, even in hindsight.

It had all started that same weekend, when she'd moved in with Charlotte. She'd spent Saturday with Will—after he'd had a long conversation with his dad—and Sunday unpacking her things, settling into her new room.

She and Charlotte had moved an old bookcase up from the

basement so she'd have a place for at least some of her books. She took her time organizing the shelf to her satisfaction, and finding other spaces to stack the rest, like in the windowsill.

As she placed some of the books that had been her father's, she couldn't help thinking of him, and what he would make of this situation. Would he be sad at what it had come to? Proud of her for standing up for herself and leaving? Disappointed at the life she'd lived since his passing? Relieved she wasn't putting up with it anymore?

She herself felt a little of each of those things.

She ran her fingers over several spines, cherishing the memory each brought before she set them on the shelf. When she came to the book of fairytales, she paused.

She'd thought of the book many times over the years, if only because the lessons her father felt could be imparted from the stories stuck with her. But she hadn't been able to look at it since he died, finding the memory too melancholy.

But now she smiled as her fingers brushed the hard, embossed cover; now the stories within held new significance.

In a way, they'd led her to Will.

So, she cracked it open, and flipped the pages until she landed on the tale of Cinderella. Maybe she'd read this one tonight, for old times' sake. She continued flipping through the pages, looking for some of her favorite illustrations, hazy in her memory.

And when she came to the last page, she froze.

There between the final page and the back cover, was an envelope. *Lizzy* was scrawled on the outside in her father's blocky handwriting.

Her fingers gripped it, but met some resistance—he'd taped it to the inside of the cover, she realized. Carefully, she pried it off and, setting the book aside, fumbled the envelope open.

She'd been expecting a letter, some last message or words of wisdom from her father. She sagged a little when she saw there were only a few lines on the crisp notebook paper.

But then the words clicked.

Lizzy, my dear, you may not understand my reasons, but I'm sure you understand what I mean when I say that even at ten, you are brighter and more responsible than your new stepmother. Though I know this method is not the most secure, I am entrusting you to safeguard this information.

Rest assured, my last will and testament, as well as other estate planning documents, are safe and sound in my study's fireproof safe. However, just in case, I've also had digital copies stored in a virtual vault. Below is the location and login information.

All my love,

Dad

Heart pounding and mind racing, Lizzy shot to her feet, snatching up her laptop and rushing into the kitchen, where Charlotte was busy cooking something. Upon seeing the look on Lizzy's face, she immediately turned off the stove.

As Charlotte read the short note, Lizzy pulled up the listed website—a secure document vault for sensitive documents. When a wide-eyed Charlotte handed the note back, she logged into the account with shaking fingers.

Naturally, what they found changed everything.

Charlotte, as she'd mentioned, had been named the executor. There was a list of things belonging to Lizzy's mother that was to go to her, but the most shocking thing was that while the house had been left to Frances, Lizzy was supposed to inherit Bookish Brews.

And at the end of the document, after her father's signature and another witness's signature—likely a notary or someone else in the law office—was Frances's sprawling, overly loopy script.

It had taken a couple months—estate law was notoriously slow moving—but with the will and her father's note, proving Frances guilty of fraud had been a relatively simple matter, which moved things along much quicker. In the end, Frances had caved and admitted to burning the hard copy of the will.

Though she knew she'd get the house, Frances knew if something happened to Thomas, she'd have to get a job. When it was assumed there was no will, she got everything—and taking control of the diner meant she could hire others to do the work, and still have an income. She hadn't wanted to give up her cushy lifestyle, or cede something she thought should be hers to a 'good-for-nothing child.'

The last thing Frances wanted was to go to prison, however, and her lawyer suggested an alternative: she would return what profits from the café she was able, and work at the café in order to pay Lizzy back in full.

For Kitty and Lydia's sake, Lizzy agreed.

Once she was officially the owner of the café, Lizzy named Charlotte her business partner, and they set about redesigning the café. Their goal was to make it look much like it had before; Lizzy felt they succeeded (Charlotte had actually rescued some of the décor and artwork and kept it in her basement), but also managed to put their own stamp on it.

They also revamped the menu, of course, which saw the return of some regulars from the café's heyday, people Lizzy only vaguely remembered from childhood. Mary was thrilled to bring back some of her favorite recipes, and experiment with new ones. Lizzy had a blast coming up with new tea blends and specialty coffees, like her father had.

It wasn't all smooth sailing, though—Frances complained as much as ever, especially about having to work. But Charlotte, still acting as manager, kept her in line.

Lydia did not take all the changes well. For a while she tried to steamroll Kitty back into their old dynamic, but Kitty, thankfully, was having none of it. She'd even gotten a job at a clothing store so she wouldn't have to rely on Frances for money.

Lydia still refused to get a job, and according to Kitty, she often argued with her and Frances about money. Kitty rarely spent much time at home anymore; Lizzy only hoped she could make it through her senior year without too much trouble.

In the midst of all this, of course, was Lizzy's developing relationship with Will. They didn't always agree on things, seeing as they were both hotheads, but being with him felt easy, and just... right. And they didn't have to worry about being separated, because they would both be attending Brown in the fall.

The lunch table that had at first felt like a hodgepodge became a solid friend group, completed with the additions of Anne's girlfriend, Jenny, and Ricky's girlfriend—none other than Kitty. The eight of them had gone to prom together, and Lizzy had taken the opportunity to wear the blue ballgown again—just like her mom.

Spring had also brought another change, as Lizzy was finally free to do something she'd longed for—try out for the softball team. She was ecstatic to make varsity, and settled in easily as their starting catcher to Jane's starting pitcher; it wasn't long before she and Jane were considered the team's power duo. Since they were done with football, Will and Charlie came to every game they could. Sometimes Will even brought Gianna, who was an even bigger supporter than her brother; and sometimes even Mrs. R came to cheer them on, ushering Robert Darcy with her.

Part of Lizzy thought it all went by too fast; another part was ready to take the next steps.

They'd walked in their graduation ceremony and received their diplomas just that morning—something Lizzy had once simply wanted to be over and done with. Now, though, she wanted to savor these last youthful memories. Though she wouldn't miss high school at all, she could appreciate the good things that happened in her last year.

And she could celebrate that good, give it the moment it deserved before moving on to the next chapter.

So, she and Charlotte had closed the café for a private graduation party. There were a couple of graduate themed balloons near the door, and Mary had cooked up a delectable spread of appetizers and treats, which had been laid out on the front counter with urns of coffee and lemonade. She, Maddie, and Ed weren't working that day, but they'd of course been invited to the party, and had commandeered one of the tables, where they chatted with Mrs. Reynolds.

Over by the big window, where she and Charlotte had set up the coziest part of Bookish Brews, Jane and Charlie sat together in a soft leather armchair, while a few of their teammates from the softball team sat across from them on the plum purple velvet sofa.

Several of the football players milled around as well, many chatting with Ricky and Kitty. Kitty had really come into her own, breaking away from the influence of her mother and sister; she even stopped straightening her hair, giving her natural curls their freedom. Though the support of all her new friends had certainly helped, much of Kitty's newfound confidence was due to Ricky and Anne.

Anne, who had a similar experience breaking with Caroline and Louisa, found a kindred spirit in Kitty, and had shared her own journey of self-discovery; the two had grown close over the past several months.

Of course, it didn't compare to the way Kitty had blossomed under Ricky's attention. Ricky, who'd never had a relationship last more than a few weeks, was smitten with her, and Kitty, who'd only experienced conditional love, was finally able to open her heart to someone who appreciated her for who she was. Thankfully, they wouldn't be too far apart next year, since Ricky was going to UCLA.

At the moment, Anne and Jenny were getting food from the counter, and at the table near the vintage hutch (the shelves of which were filled with books), Robert and Gianna Darcy sat playing a game of chess.

There was another big change, Lizzy noted. Robert was spending more quality time with his family, even making sure to be home for dinner every evening.

Once he'd gotten over being upset at Will's decision not to go to Stanford, and accepted Will didn't want to join the family business, he'd felt guilty his son hadn't felt like he could share his true aspirations with him. That he hadn't seen Will's hesitation.

Feeling like he didn't know his own children was a powerful motivator for Robert to spend more time with them, and talk *to* them instead of *at* them. He was now a staunch Brown supporter, and Will was a lot calmer and less stressed than he was in his closeted Closet Poet days.

Lizzy slid her arm around Will's waist and snuggled closer.

"Well, don't you two look cute and cuddly," Charlotte teased as she came up beside them.

Lizzy smirked. "I'm just soaking it all in. This whole party is evidence of how much has changed."

Charlotte nodded, and looked around at all the party guests. "Sometimes I catch myself just staring at everything, and I think I should pinch myself to make sure it's real."

With subtle motion, Will moved his fingers to lightly pinch Lizzy's arm.

"Hey!" She poked him in the sternum. "*I* didn't say I needed a pinch."

"Yeah, but maybe I wanted to make sure you were real."

"That's not how it works." The stern look she tried to give him was belied by her smile.

Enjoying them, Charlotte nodded to Will. "The sound system is on, if you're ready."

Lizzy drew back a bit to give him and Charlotte a curious look. "Ready for what?"

"You'll see," Will said, letting her go and walking over to the little stage in the corner. He stepped onto it and turned the mic on, clearing his throat.

"Hey, everybody. Thanks for coming."

He shuffled his feet a little; obviously he was still a bit uncomfortable on the stage, though he'd been on it many times in recent months. One of the changes Lizzy had been adamant on making to the café was to reinstate their open mic nights, and she'd managed to convince Will to read some of his poetry during the first one.

She thought she'd have to push him a little, but once he warmed to the idea, he was all in. He'd read one of his poems at nearly every open mic, despite not particularly enjoying being the center of attention.

And he did draw attention—a few times he'd posted about his readings on his Closet Poet account, and the café had gotten plenty of new patrons. Clearly, Closet Poet had somewhat of a fan base going, and as a surprise for him, she'd had the mask poem he'd texted her styled into an art print, framed, and hung on the art wall in the café.

"It's been a hell of a year," Will continued, "and to commemorate the occasion, I wanted to share a little something I've learned over the past several months. It might be a little corny, but..."

He pulled a folded piece of notebook paper from his pocket, opened it, and with a shy glance at Lizzy, read:

"A fairytale's true magic
is its ability to span the ages
for we find within its pages
a kind of certainty.
It's timeless in its comfort
and the lessons it imparts—
opening minds, opening hearts—
holding up a mirror
to the truth behind the lie
and the masks we hide behind
for all the world to see.
And a lot of people say
fairytales don't come true;
but I don't agree
because I know mine is you."

As he folded the paper back up, their little party broke into enthusiastic applause. Will blushed a little, and said, "Thank you. I don't know where I'd be without any of you, but especially you, Lizzy. I'll always be grateful to you for changing my life."

"Here here!" Charlie called, lifting his glass of lemonade, which of course provoked a chorus of "here here's" from around the room. Will didn't have a glass in his hand, so he simply nodded in acknowledgement, and stepped off the stage.

Lizzy's heart was utter mush by the time he returned to her. "Will, that was..."

"I know, I know. Super cheesy."

"Yes," she beamed, "but in the best way possible. Thank you."

"You're welcome."

"Well, since you've decided to one up me, I suppose I might as well give you your present."

He raised a brow as she went behind the counter, came back with a book-sized package wrapped in silvery paper.

"Should I open it now?"

"Duh," she said as he took it.

Grinning at her, he tore gently at the paper, and revealed a leather-bound journal with thick pages, and his favorite brand of ball point pen. His heart swelled with love for her, and her quietly thoughtful gestures.

"For your poems, obviously," she said, a little quiver in her voice giving away her nerves. "When I saw it, it just kind of screamed 'Will needs me!'"

"It's awesome," he said, pulling the rest of the paper away. "Thank you."

He set the gift and the paper aside, then turned to wrap her up in a long, hard hug. When he pulled back to take her in, look into her deep blue-violet eyes, she pinked a little under his steady gaze.

"I can't wait to start the next chapter of our lives," he murmured.

She knew he was thinking of Brown, and being on the complete opposite side of the country from their friends and family. It was a little nerve wracking, but she knew he was just as excited as she was. It would be an entirely new experience, but they'd have each other.

"Me either," she said.

Grinning, he gave her a quick kiss—a small preview of the kisses she knew they'd share later, when they had time alone.

This was her life now, she mused as they enjoyed the rest of the party. A year ago, she would never have thought any of this possible; she'd simply wanted to keep her head down and escape. Now, for the first time in years, she had a real home—a place she wanted to return to—and she was truly happy.

She still missed her dad, and she always would, but she knew he'd approve of the family she'd made. He'd tried to give her one by marrying Frances, and in a roundabout way, it had led her to the people she loved most.

Of course, it was impossible to tell what the future had in store, but she had faith in her happily ever after.

She'd certainly earned it.

Author's Note

If you've seen *A Cinderella Story*, you know baseball and the quote "Never let the fear of striking out keep you from playing the game," are significant to Sam and her dad; he even had the quote printed on the wall of Hal's Diner. It's a great quote, but I've always found it odd it wasn't attributed to anyone, especially since the great Babe Ruth is credited with that nugget of wisdom.

Although accounts vary whether the aforementioned quote is the true one, or if it's "Never let the fear of striking out get in your way," (or both), it is, either way, sage advice. I chose to use the first quote in the epigraph because it's a tie to *A Cinderella Story*—a fun allusion for fans of the movie.

I've been sitting on the idea of a reverse Cinderella scenario, in which the prince knew Cinderella was Elizabeth, but she didn't know the prince was Darcy, and I finally decided to tackle it. Eventually, I realized a mashup with *A Cinderella Story* was the perfect way to modernize it.

I remember when *A Cinderella Story* came out; I loved it when I first saw it, and it's still a nostalgic, light-hearted watch for me. However, I am aware it has its flaws, and so I endeavored to change or correct them to the best of my ability, using elements from each story to create a whole new story. I hope I succeeded.

A heartfelt thanks to my readers for reading! Sharing my stories with you makes it all worth it.

—*Mac*

Also by McKinley James

A Turn of Events

Netherfield Vacation

Vitriol and Vineyards

Seaglass and Simplicity

My Reluctant Roommate

A Tale of Mistletoe Shenanigans

Snowed In

In the Stacks

Down the Heart

Collections:

Incandescently

About the Author

Of all Austen's characters, McKinley James identifies most with the quiet, socially awkward, and introverted Darcy. Pride and Prejudice is an old friend, and upon discovering the vast and fascinating world of Jane Austen Fan Fiction (and subsequently journeying down a year-long JAFF reading rabbit-hole) she decided to toss her own P&P stories into the fray. McKinley has a bachelor's degree in Creative Writing and, in her other life, works at a library. She lives in Chicago.

www.mckinleyjameswrites.com

www.ingramcontent.com/pod-product-compliance
Lightning Source LLC
Chambersburg PA
CBHW020106180626
46812CB00006B/2486